My Son's Best Friend

Christine Massa

Contents

Chapter 1

It was the middle of the day when I received the unexpected call that would shatter my heart into a thousand pieces. After almost a year of calculating lies and deceit Daniel had finally slipped up and left his phone unlocked letting himself get caught by his girlfriend, the one I didn't know about.

"Hello," an unfamiliar but local number flashed on my phone.

"Is this Mia?" A woman on the other end asked.

"Yes, this is her. Who's this?" I was completely baffled and curious as to who the hell this woman was and how she knew me.

"This is Daniel's girlfriend," I'd never had a knife pierced into my chest before but at that moment I had a good idea what it felt like.

We would go on to speak for over an hour sobbing to each other trading stories of our betrayal. I had come to learn from our conversation she wasn't just Daniel's girlfriend, she was now his fiance. It felt like someone had reached into my chest squeezing my heart so tight it was about to explode. The signs were always there but I ignored them, it was so much easier to keep lying to myself then accepting the truth. The pain was almost unbearable but I realized I could never be with someone like him, the revelation didn't help ease my pain though.

I needed to forget, find some way to sooth my suffering. I was ready to do something reckless and stupid, I needed to feel wanted if only for the night. I knew once I got a little alcohol in me I wouldn't care so much so I straightened my long black hair, threw on some make-up, a cute blouse , jeans, and 2 inch platforms to give my short 5'4 frame some height and headed to the bar.

A couple of men hit on me while I sat alone drinking but the beer goggles hadn't taken effect yet to find any of them the least bit attractive. I got up from the bar stool and made my way to the ladies room for the third time since I had been there. I had the tolerance of a lumberjack but the bladder the size of a pea.

I was almost there but a tall handsome figure blocked my path, at least he looked handsome from behind standing there talking to his buddies. I couldn't help but check him out from the back, he had silky dark black hair with broad shoulders and an ass so tight he could probably shoot a diamond out of it.

"Excuse me," I uttered over the blaring music trying to wedge my way past him.

He quickly whipped around accidentally knocking my drink out of my hand with his elbow.

"Fuck!" I yelled out with the alcohol soaking into my shirt and dripping down my jeans. I could feel the uncomfortable wetness against my chest looking down pulling my blouse off of my skin. Great, I looked like I was getting ready to enter a wet t-shirt contest.

"I'm so sorry, let me buy you another one,"apologetically he was now facing me and my brown eyes were in awe at the sight of him looking up. He was strikingly good looking with a sculpted jawline, his eyes were a shade of teal blue that pierced right through me with his stare, and his body was a thick muscular work of art with massive bulging biceps hugging the seams of his sleeves. All of a sudden I didn't seem to care so much that you could see my hard nipples peering through my white shirt.

"Y..ea sure, l- let me clean up first." I found it hard to get the words out of my mouth he was so intimidatingly handsome.

"Okay, I'll wait for you at the bar. Again, I'm really sorry." his husky voice sending shooting sparks down between my legs.

I went into the bathroom relieving my tiny bladder and then moved to the sink soaping up some paper towels. I tried washing up as much as possible with the little resources I had in a hurry so I could talk to the gorgeous stranger. He was breath taking but he was also only about twenty five which was ten years my junior making me question if it was such a good idea. He was only a couple of years older then my son, should I really be doing this? Screw it, we were both adults. Hollywood stars married or dated people young enough to be their grandchildren, why can't I have a little fun after what I'd been through today. It's not like I hadn't dated men that young before.

I touched up my lip gloss, perked up my 34C's, and went over to the bar taking the empty seat next to this handsome stranger. "So where did all your friends go?" I noticed when I came out that all his buddies had disappeared. "Someone's a little confident aren't they?" I teased like I actually wasn't going to leave with him which I damn well knew I was. Yes I was a sure thing for him tonight but I was still going to put up a fight.

"It's not like that," he smirked letting out a slight laugh. "They wanted to go to another bar and I owed you a drink so I told them to go without me." Then he raked his fingers through his hair pushing it out of his face exposing his mesmerizing gaze.

"Sure," I nodded my head with attitude. "I'm much older than you, I know a thing or two when it comes to the male libido."

"Oh come on, don't you trust me and you don't look but a couple of years older than me?" Ha, that's what he thought. I was fortunate to have aged well always fooling people but I was much older then I looked and of course I didn't trust him. If you were at a bar with a penis in between your legs you were untrustworthy.

"Cosmo," I lightly changed the subject. His question bared an obvious answer and I didn't want to scare him off if he really did know how old I was not that it actually mattered. His decision was made, I was who he wanted to take home tonight and I was easily willing. Oh these little games we play were always the same leading up to the inevitable, sex.

"Ha? Oh, your drink. Gotcha," and then he raised his hand gesturing for the bartender. "Cosmo please."

The bartender complied hastily placing the drink by my mystery man's hand in less then a minute.

"So what's your name?" he asked handing me my beverage.

"I'd prefer to keep things simple if I do decide I want to go home with you tonight. No names," I shrugged my shoulders head nodding, "let's just have some fun." Well I pretty much just admitted he was getting laid tonight but I didn't want to get personal. It's not like we were ever going to see each other again after tonight.

"Then what do I call you?" He inched in closer to me placing his hand on my thigh squeezing in and out. His massaging fingers felt so good rubbing against me igniting heated flames inside my body.

"Does it really matter?" I moved in lapping my tongue over his lip licking and then biting down. He tasted so divine I wanted more almost ravaging him right there at the bar.

He brought his hand up cupping my cheek kissing me back roughly, "You're a naughty girl aren't you?" he momentarily broke away whispering through parted lips by the lobe of my ear. His rasped manly voice and heated breath caused me to shiver it was so enticing.

"Buy me a couple more drinks and maybe I'll let you find out later," I seductively taunted rubbing my hand in the crotch of his jeans over top his soft member feeling it start to awaken. Call me a slut but the feel of him hardening beneath turned me on.

He just smirked the evilest of grins and then ordered me another drink.

After a few more Cosmos I was feeling pretty loose and horny. Nothing mattered anymore except the idea of doing very bad things with the god that sat before me. I was drunk but not to where I was slurring or unable to make conscious decisions. I knew exactly what I was doing, somehow this young man eased my pain making me forget my woes at the same time arousing my sexual desires.

We sat there for about an hour or so more flirting and teasing each other until neither one of us could keep our hands to ourselves.

"Your place or mine?," he asked with one hand under my shirt trickling up to my breast before he kissed me harshly with his other hand tugging behind my hair.

I struggled to contain myself clutching my thighs together hard trying to fight off that tingling sensation that yearned for entrance in between my legs. "Your place," if we went to my house he would definitely run at the sight of my homely house and family photos plastered all over.

I left my car in the parking lot and following him to his vehicle parked a row away. It's not like I would have been able to drive anyway with the amount of alcohol I had consumed.

"Are you okay to drive? Maybe we should just call a cab," I was all for going home with him but I was against drunk driving as we made our way to his silver Escalade.

"I've only had two and a half beers tonight. I'm completely sober," I guess I was too busy drowning my sorrows in alcohol and being sexual aroused I ignored to notice that he was barely drinking. I was able to notice though how when he replied the corner of his mouth pinched up to his cheek with a charismatic smile that had me craving for his moist lips all over me.

"Oh," was the only response I could muster up as I took a seat on the black leather interior.

We got to his apartment and began tearing into each other the moment we stepped foot through the doorway.

He crossed his arms and grabbed the hems of his shirt pulling it over his head and tossing it to the floor. I took that as my cue to remove my shirt letting my bra follow behind it. A small squeal of delight left me at the sight of his flawless naked upper body. My eyes followed down to the hairless v-line just above his jeans. By this point I think I was starting to drool.

I had no self control left in me, I started nibbling and licking his lips until his mouth parted and our tongues met. We kissed intensely until I pulled away biting and sliding my tongue around his neck slowly making my way down. When I reached his nipples I sucked swirling my tongue taking tiny bites. A small groan escaped him as he let me have my way.

When I reached his jeans I didn't undo them immediately. I teased and taunted never letting my mouth fall below the seams. His flesh heated and his body trembled nervously anticipating my next move.

He groaned some more taking my hair in his fingers tightening his grip and tugging hard. "Please I can't take it, I want to f*ck your mouth," desperation echoed in his tone.

I looked up into his pleading eyes with a devilish smirk, "What? You want me to go further?"

"You enjoy making me suffer don't you?"

"Just a little," I cringed winking an eye at him. I took his hand in mine and walked us over to the sofa. With his back facing the cushions I undid his jeans taking them down to his knees and then shoved him down to the couch.

I reveled at the sight of his over sized large member, it was so thick and long my mouth watered for a taste. I took the head of it into my mouth with my hand stroking the shaft. I playfully kept my lips no lower than the tip swirling and sucking at the head until finally I inhaled him completely in one quick motion. He started thrusting his hips holding my head tight forcing himself down my throat. Impatiently he hammered into my mouth until I found myself gagging several times from taking in such a large prize. Saliva and his juices dripped from my chin as my fingers continued to tug at his skin with my lips wrapped around him.

I clenched my thighs in again trying to restrain my sex while it screamed out wanting to be violated. Giving him pleasure was such a turn on.

"Fuck! You feel so fucking good," he called out pulling my face up for a hard kiss.

He slipped his legs out of the bottom of his jeans and scooped me up in his arms carrying me off to the bedroom. Angrily he threw me down on my back side removing the rest of my clothing with one quick tug. My arousal increased as he handled me roughly.

He hovered above me placing my left nipple in his mouth sucking hard. One of his hands found it's way to my right breast squeezing in and out as his other fell between my fold. His fingers rubbed inside my soaking with lips making circles around my cl*t.

"Mmmm yes," I groaned with his fingers finding their way inside me thrusting in and out. Faster and faster they moved making me have to bite down on my lip trying to contain myself.

He took turns on each breast toying with my nipples sucking and biting. Fuck me, I wanted him so badly I decided to stroke him some more so I could feel his hard stiffness. My entire body was in flames I was so heated gasping and panting in pleasure.

"Fuck me now," I demanded digging my nails into his back. My body couldn't take it anymore, I needed to feel him inside of my depths.

He reached over on the nightstand grabbing the small foil wrapper tearing it open and placing on the rubber. Anxiously I awaited until I felt his hard tip slowly making its way into my entrance. I began to melt once he fully made his way in with my walls tightening around.

Slowly he began thrusting gradually increasing his speed with one arm hovered over me pressing on the mattress for support. His other hand moved down rubbing my cl*t with his fingers circling around vigorously. I locked my legs around his waist clutching onto his *ss cheeks so I could shove him into me as far as he could go.

"Oh God!" I screamed out as the sensations flowing through me rocked me to the core.

" I want to turn over, "I told him in between pants gasping for breath. I loved being pounded from behind.

"You're full of surprises aren't you?," he agreed happily flipping me over on all fours and then shoved himself deep inside me again this time without the slow strides. Promptly he was thrusting with the same precision as before but I wanted and needed more.

"I want you to spank me and f*ck me harder," I pleaded.

"That's my bad girl,"he dominantly said and without hesitation he hammered into me as hard as he could slapping my ass several times in between thrusts.

"Ummm," I moaned quivering from the sharp sting that burned my dairy air but at the same time brought me to heightening pleasures.

"Is this how you like it baby?" He held onto both *ss cheeks firmly smacking my right side a few more times.

"Oh god yes, don't stop," he was hitting right into my *-spot taking me to unknown places that I didn't want to come back from.

"You're so wet baby girl, your hot p*ssy feels amazing wrapped around my d*ck," he uttered in between pounding strokes.

He twisted my hair around his hand tugging my head back until I faced him and then he started kissing me fiercely. He kept grinding into me with full force bringing me closer to satisfaction until I screamed out in pure delight. I kept going until he let out a loud moan of completion and fell down rolling over besides me.

"What is it about you?" he asked kissing down on my breasts. I just lay back sprawled out running my fingers through his soft hair unsure what he was asking.

"What do you mean?" I questioned.

"I don't know what it is but I find you irresistible and the sex was unbelievable. Can I see you again after tonight?"

"Why don't we discuss it in the morning?", and then I planted a soft kiss on his lips before rolling over with the blanket in my hand going to sleep.

I passed out immediately not hearing his response if he had given one until I saw daylight cracking through his bedroom window. I looked over and he was sound asleep. I quietly tiptoed around collecting my clothes and got dressed as fast as possible before I woke him. I walked outside until I made it a few blocks away calling a cab waiting at the curb.

My heart still ached over Daniel but not as harshly as it first did. Somehow I couldn't stop thinking about my young suitor and the night we just had. Oh well, it's not like I was ever going to see him again but at least he left me with a night I'd never forget.

Chapter 2

I woke up with my head throbbing from being so drunk last night vaguely remembering my actions but I recalled enough. Oh shit! I fucked some boy, well technically a man, but he was a boy to me considering he could be just a couple of years older than my son.

Somehow I couldn't forget how our hot bodies collided bringing me to a state of ecstasy. Seriously, how could I feel this way about some stranger I just met that night? I thought forgetting about Daniel was going to be harder but after being with him my pain subsided quicker than I imagined. Don't get me wrong, it still hurt. I thought I was in love with Daniel but it turned out I didn't even know him. He had a whole other life he kept hidden from me. I knew the pain wasn't going to go away in one night but letting loose had eased some of my suffering.

My head was still spinning so I reached over and grabbed the bottle of Excedrin I kept on my nightstand, taking two pills to the bathroom with me so I could get a glass of water. I stumbled back to my bed after I swallowed the pills and lay back down for a nap. It was going to take at least thirty minutes before my head stopped spinning and I wanted to make sure I wasn't too sluggish and unresponsive when Tyler got home.

It had been two weeks since I had last seen my baby boy, well not so much a baby anymore, he was twenty now but he'd always be my little boy no matter how old he was. I was only fifteen when I had him so of course me and his father didn't last but we both raised him and split custody. Even though Tyler was a grown man now he still stayed with me most of the time because he was attending Towson State University only twenty minutes from our home. It was summer break right now and Tyler spent the last several weeks with his father doing some male bonding but he was coming back here today.

I slept for about two hours feeling more alive and less hungover than I did when I first woke up. Tyler would be arriving in another hour or so, so I got up and went to the bathroom to shower. I undressed setting the water to the perfect temperature and then got settled in letting the heated waters sooth my skin. Quickly I shampooed and conditioned my hair then lathered my body rinsing off. I got out drying off as fast as possible because I wanted to have lunch ready for Tyler as soon as he walked through the front door. He loved my homemade lasagna and it took me about fifty minutes to make so I had to hustle throwing my clothes on before I had fully dried up.

I used my wet dry curling iron to straighten and dry my hair real quick and then tied it up in a ponytail since I was about to cook. I had thrown on my red floral sundress with spaghetti straps since it was comfortable and easy.

I got down to the kitchen and pulled out all my ingredients from the cabinet and the refrigerator. I started preparing everything heating up the oven and getting out my skillet to cook the meats. Once that was done I drained it out putting it in a bowl with the Ricotta cheese and mixed everything up ready to lay out in the pan with the sauce and noodles. I put on the finishing touches topping it off with sauce and mozzarella in a hurry getting the lasagna in the oven in fifteen minutes. Perfect, it would be fresh and hot just in time. Right while I was placing it on the rack I heard Tyler coming in the front door, shit he was early. I guess he was just going to have to wait to eat, it didn't really matter that much anyways, I was just glad he was finally home.

"Sweety did you have a good time with your father?" I yelled making my way out the kitchen towards the dining room so I could greet him with open arms.

"Yea, it was fun. I have a buddy with me. He's staying for lunch. Mom this is my friend Jayce Montgomery," Tyler announced entering through the front door standing tall with his large build, ruffled brown hair, and sparkling brown eyes I missed and loved.

Instead of hugging him I stopped dead in my tracks turning a pale sheet of white when I saw who came walking up behind him. Oh god what did I do?! I looked down at the floor waiting to see it start cracking because I was sure at any second it was going to split open and suck me down to hell for what I had just done.

Jayce looked over when he entered recognizing me instantly. I knew because the same horror that met my face met his when he saw me standing there frozen. How could it be? The handsome stranger with jet black hair and striking features I had expected never to see again came striding in my front doors and with my son!

Fuck! How could this be happening to me? I stood there stiffly in shock unable to speak for a moment. I could feel panic sweep through me not knowing what to do or say next.

"Mom, you okay? You look like you've just seen a ghost," Tyler asked with the most baffled look on his face sitting his bags down on the floor.

"Um..um, yea. I'm fine baby. I just wasn't expecting you to have company with you," I shook it off hugging Tyler before I looked over to Jayce with a forced smile.

"So nice to meet you Jayce. I'm Mia Sheperd, Tyler's mom," I nodded acknowledging him trying hard not to arouse any more suspicion. I had already screwed up with my initial reaction to seeing Jayce, I didn't want Tyler to suspect anything. I could already feel the sweat beading above my brows I was so nervous Tyler would know something. He could never find out his mother had sex with one of his friend, it would break his heart.

"Nice to meet you to Ms. Sheperd," Jayce responded recomposed like he hadn't just fucked my brains out last night.

"Mom prefers that my friends call her by her first name. It reminds her too much how old she is if you call her Ms. Sheperd," Tyler chuckled looking over to Jayce.

I smacked Tyler on the shoulder with the outside of my hand, "Haha, I'm not that old kid," I retorted not truly taking offense to his remark. He loved joking about my age because he knew the idea of being considered old bothered the hell out of me.

"Ouch," Tyler chuckled rubbing just above his arm where I had hit him.

"I think your mom looks pretty young," Jayce politely spoke giving me an intense stare that could burn right through metal. God he was gorgeous having me briefly hypnotized as his eyes stung through me.

At that moment the timer for the lasagna went off saving me from coming up with a response. "I've got to take the foil off the top of the lasagna so the cheese will cook evenly and I need to prepare the salad. You boys go watch television while I finish making lunch." I tried making a fast getaway but Jayce wasn't trying to make it that easy for me.

"I'll go help your mom in the kitchen. Why don't you go take your bags upstairs and get yourself re-situated while I help out?" Jayce turned to face Tyler pretending to be all innocent but I knew what devilish evils he was capable of, he showed me that last night.

"It's okay, I'm fine. You boys should relax, I've got this," I tried to persuade but Jayce was more than persistent.

"Oh no, I insist, I want to help," a large grin shined across his diabolical face.

"Mom when do you ever turn down help from me or my friends? You're usually bitching that we don't do enough to help out. You sure you're okay?"

"Yea, I'm fine," I laughed flinging my hand up in the air like Tyler was out of his mind. "I just missed my wittle baby," I said in gibberish squeezing his face together so his lips puckered and then I planted a big wet kiss on the side of his face.

"Yea, you're fine," he rolled his eyes at me pulling back. "I'm going to unpack while you guys take care of the food," Tyler reached over picking up his bags going downstairs to his room only to leave me alone with Jayce.

As soon as we got in the kitchen I turned around in anger facing Jayce halting him in his tracks. "Did you know who I was in the bar, is this some sick game to you?" I didn't know what to think as our faces stood only inches away while I slightly began to tremble in his presence I could still feel the heat between us.

"No, of course not. I had no clue who you were when I met you. What we did wasn't wrong though, we're both grown-ups. It's messed up you had to be Tyler's mom but I'm also glad because I thought I would never see you again," he placed his hand over top of my hand sitting on the counter and started caressing my skin. I could feel the electricity course through when our flesh met once again, momentarily forgetting that he just came in with Tyler minutes ago.

"No, what we did was wrong. You're like what twenty, twenty-one? You're just a kid," I jerked my hand back snapping out the trance he had just put me under.

Jayce grabbed me by my waist pinning me up against the counter. He brought his mouth in real close to my ear I could feel his hot breath emunating onto neck. "I'm twenty-three, I'm a grown man and I know what I want, I want you," he whispered sending shivers up and down my spine causing me to take in a deep gulp nervously shaking.

"Th..th..this is wrong," I stuttered quivering apprehensive but yet excited by him. I could feel the moisture start to accumulate between my legs while he stood so close holding me in his grips. He was turning me on and I couldn't seem to conceal it.

He reached under the hem of my dress sliding his fingers inside my panties until he was playing with my seeping clit. He began circling his fingers around the pink flesh causing more moisture to accumulate. I was so wet I could hear my juices squishing around under his dominance.

"See, you can't deny it, you're soaked and I just started touching you," and then he shoved two fingers up in me thrashing hard in and out pumping my pussy.

"Please, you need to stop," I moaned but he kept fucking me with his fingers ignoring all my pleas.

"You don't really want me to stop. You want me just as badly as I want you naughty girl," he lapped his tongue across my bottom lip then took it into his mouth sucking softly.

My eyes closed with my hands clutching hard onto the counter for leverage panting and moaning. I didn't know how to stop him, my body wouldn't let me all heated up yearning for more.

"Hey mom, is lunch ready," I heard Tyler yell coming up the steps heading towards the kitchen, startling the both of his.

Jayce pulled his fingers out of me taking a step back, I quickly turned my backside to him grabbing my mitts and going over to the oven. Damn that was close.

"Just a little bit longer," I replied bent over pulling the lasagna half way out of the oven so I could remove the foil covering. Jayce had moved over standing off by the sink washing his hands.

I got up and looked over at Tyler, "Why don't you go set the table? The foods almost done. Jayce here was getting ready to finish chopping up the lettuce for the salad weren't you?," I veered my face in the direction of Jayce giving him a stern look.

"Yes ma'am," Jayce grinned walking over to the cutting board taking the knife in his hand.

With Tyler only feet away Jayce maintained his good behavior for the rest of the time he was in the kitchen. I kept quiet afraid

Tyler might overhear something he shouldn't. Luckily Jayce didn't say anything else either.

I brought the lasagna to the dining room table, Jayce followed behind with the salad bowl and we all took a seat for lunch.

"So how do you two know each other, why haven't I ever had the pleasure of meeting Jayce before?" Tyler didn't often bring his friends home he was always so out and about so I was curious when this friendship started and how long they had been hanging out. I was hoping they weren't that good of friends but I wasn't that fortunate.

"Jayce goes to school with me, were both in the same business class. We usually hang out at his apartment but a water main busted in the building and he has no hot water for a little while. It's going to be a couple of weeks until he can move back in." Tyler replied taking the fork to his mouth with a large chunk of pasta.

"So where is Jayce staying now?" I felt an empty pit burrow in my stomach when I asked that question with the feeling I wasn't going to be to happy with the answer I was about to get.

"Mommy," Tyler put on his sweet baby face, "you know I love you so so much right?" Oh god, here it comes.

"What do you want Tyler," I cringed placing my fork down. I knew that face and voice all too well, it was that " I need something from you" look and tone.

"I told Jayce he could stay here with us in the spare bedroom until his place is fixed up. That's cool right?" Tyler nonchalantly questioned unaware of the predicament he was putting me in.

"You won't even notice I'm here. I'll make sure I stay out of your way Mia," It seemed like he took pleasure in that lie and saying my name out loud since I wouldn't give it to him. This kid was something else. Kid, he was a kid and he had been spanking me, Jesus, the irony in that was so humiliating.

What could I say? I couldn't say no or Tyler would definitely become suspicious. I had already been acting weird enough today for him to notice there was something wrong. Shit! I was so screwed, the extra room was directly next to mine and it had a joining door to my bedroom. I had it put in when Tyler was little and used that room as his nursery. I've always been a paranoid mother, it took me until he was fifteen to finally get use to him crossing the street by himself and even then I was still worried he would forget to look both ways.

"Of course you're little friend can stay," I said teasingly knowing damn well the boy was far from little. Joking seemed to be the only way to mask my overwhelming fear that no good could come from this. I of course didn't think that one threw until after I said it making me only more apprehensive.

"Thanks mom."

"Thank you Mia."

"Can you two put all this away when you're done? I think you were right Tyler, I am feeling a bit off today. I think I might be coming down with something, I should go lay down for a little while if you guys don't mind." If I stayed down there any longer I was going to give something away and I knew it. First I find out Daniel's a serious piece of shit, then I find out I fucked my son's best friend, and now he's going to be living with me for a couple of weeks! I was seriously ready to pass out from all the shock. I needed to lay down and pretend like this was all just one bad dream.

"We've got this, right Tyler?," Jayce spoke nodding his head never taking his eyes off of me with a smile so wide it spread cheek to cheek.

"Yea, go lay down ma, get some rest."

"Thanks," I got up from my seat abruptly and went upstairs to my bedroom.

CHAPTER 3

I sat there perched on the sofa having a conversation with my best friend over the phone. I was basically arguing with her trying to get her not to come over.

Jayce had now been living here for a week and I had successfully avoided either seeing him or being left alone in a room with him if we were home at the same time. Most of the time I hid out at my web design company. I had started it while I was in my early twenties and had now established it to where I didn't really need to work if I didn't want to. It was a small business but I had enough faithful employees to run it in my absence and it paid the bills with a decent amount leftover to live comfortably.

I had also kept Beth away from him in fear that she would let something slip or just humiliate me. She was that one best friend that you confided everything to, not that I as a female could have been able to keep that dirty secret all to myself. Sex that amazing with such a youthful Adonis was way too juicy to not share.

I think she also liked living vicariously through me even though she was a year younger than myself. Beth never had men looking at her the way they stared at me. She had made the mistake at a young age to frequently use tanning beds which only aged her appearance. It made her look like a wrinkled prune at thirty-four. You could tell underneath she use to be quite beautiful with her thick natural blonde hair, hourglass figure, and emerald green eyes but ruined it with the fears of trying to hold onto her youth. She had accomplished the opposite by destroying her skin from lying under florescent tubes year after year.

I had been fortunate enough to have a natural olive skin tone never needing or wanting to tan. I was half Asian and half Irish somehow having the end results of looking Hispanic. People were constantly mistaking my nationality speaking to me in Spanish. My response would always be, Huh?" with my jaw dropped and a dumbfounded expression covering my face. That usually seemed to get them to start speaking English instead and realize I was a different nationality.

When I was a teenager I worked part time in the mall at a wireless company selling cell phones in a highly populated Hispanic area. I would be approached at least once a day by someone trying to talk to me in a foreign language. My co-workers found it amusing even making a Maria name tag instead of my actual name for fun. Every once in awhile I would wear it just for kicks to see what kind of reactions I could get. The best one was when I did my stupefied, "Huh?" and the man looked down pointing at my name tag, "but Maria?" he spoke with his strong accent looking completely boggled. My reaction was, "Yeah, still not Spanish dude."

My younger sister came off looking Italian not having to endure the constant hola's and explaining her heritage like I did. God really works in mysterious ways. Some siblings can come off looking almost identical where in our situation we didn't even look related. I was pissed when she stole my Id and got it taken. Bouncers don't wear beer goggles little sis, that's only reserved for the people in the bar not the ones standing at the door.

Now back to Beth. She had been nagging me all week to see Jayce in person since I had described him to her and the experience that we had shared. When I told her that he was staying here for awhile she literally started making her way to her car to drive over until I was able to talk her out of coming over. It would have looked really peculiar for one of my friends to stop over on a weeknight at 11:30 pm considering I had actually been going into work all week. Beth didn't need an excuse for being up and about during all hours not needing rest. She was currently separated from her fourth husband living relaxed with no job strictly off of alimony checks. It was because she liked to frequently marry and divorce so often that led us to meeting. I had met her through her second husband. Michael was one of my first employees but eventually left when his relationship crumbled with Beth and mine and hers flourished. It was too uncomfortable for him to have his boss be buddy buddy with his ex-wife so he resigned and went to another company.

No! You're not coming over," I yelled out objectively with Beth still at the other end.

"He's at the house now isn't he?" she asked with enthusiasm.

"Mom, seriously Daniel's not worth all the stress. You haven't lit up in months." Tyler had come downstairs, Jayce right behind him, finding me sitting on the sofa smoking a cigarette with the phone up to my ear. If he had only knew the stress of Daniel breaking my heart didn't nearly compare to the stress I felt for possibly breaking his if I continued this forbidden fling.

"I told you, I don't need new car insurance!" I yelled through the line.

"You're young stud muffins standing right by you isn't he?" Beth giddishly responded through the other end with excitement.

"Good Day!" and then I hung up. "Sorry baby, I've got these telemarketers harassing me constantly and then there's the whole Daniel thing on top of it. I know how much you hate smoking and worry about my health. I promise I'll keep it down to a minimal." Yes! They didn't overhear my conversation with Beth and I totally played that off.

"Who's Daniel?" Jayce curiously jumped in taking a seat in the recliner across from me.

"This two timing creep that my mom just broke up with," Tyler said to Jayce before looking at me with concern. I know he wanted to make sure I wasn't too upset discussing Daniel so shortly after being deceived by the man I thought I was going to spend the rest of my life with.

I didn't get the opportunity to reply, my phone started blowing up first ringing, that I ignored, and then the beeping texts started to chime in when I rejected the calls. Beth could be so relentless.

"Oooh," Tyler cooed crouched over the sofa bending down trying to catch a glimpse of my screen to see who was lighting up my cell. "Did we interrupt you talking dirty and sexting a new guy? Are you just stressing cause there's a new man already?" Tyler playfully teased. We had more of a brother and sister relationship then we did mother and son. I was so young when I had him I was no good at disciplining considering I was a kid myself when I got pregnant.

The only thing that was different from being siblings was he was my world, I loved him more than I could love anyone in my entire life. We love our parents, our brothers and sisters, but once you have a child of your own you experience a love that can't compare to any other.

"You're mom's a beautiful woman and she looks much too young to have a twenty year old son. It's not shocking that she has many admirers," Jayce defended me but sounded depressed, like I sensed jealousy in his voice. Na, no way but his words were hard not to take complimenting causing me to blush a little.

Tyler stood up from his hunching stance over the sofa standing stiffly looking eye to eye at Jayce, "You're not hitting on my mom are you? Cause if you are I'm going to have to kick your ass bro."

"I'm just telling it how it is. Your moms is hot and you know it but you're her son so I understand you feel protective but we're all adults here." I could see exactly what Jayce was doing, he was gradually but inconspicuously trying to win Tyler's approval but I knew my son and that would never fly. I did totally become soaked at him calling me hot though.

"We may be adults but she's my mom and you're my friend. Chill," anger and frustration could be heard in Tyler's tone with him holding a look of death on his face. Fuck me in the ass with a steel pole right now! It would be less painful then Tyler finding out the truth and the worst part is even if he knew, I don't know how I would be able to stop with Jayce defiantly pursuing me. He had some kind of hold on me I'd never felt before and something in me just couldn't say no when he was around. Verbally the words might have come out but every other part of me didn't comply to the words I spoke outloud when it came to Jayce. Fuck, fuck, fuck, vagina, fuck! I was doomed to the pits of hell. I think I saw the floor starting to crack again ready to take me but I don't recall selling my soul. Oh yea, I did that already when I fucked Jayce, his dick in my vajj was me signing on the dotted line.

"Hey, calm down. We're just talking man. It's not like I'm the devil's spawn. Weren't you heading out to your car anyways to go grab your xbox so we could play Call of Duty?" Somehow Jayce had distracted Tyler's protectiveness and strayed him off in another direction.

"Yea, I forgot that's the whole reason we came downstairs in the first place," you could still see the rage slightly protruding from Tyler's facial expressions but he left things at that and grabbed his keys off the rack stepping outside to get to his car.

"Really Jayce? You see how much this upsets Tyler and he doesn't even know the details about me and you. I thought you were his friend? Can't you see by now from all the time you've spent with us how much I love him? I would do anything for him. Why can't you just leave things alone?" I was frustrated and confused making eye contact with Jayce which was another thing I had avoided. Whenever our eyes met I would fall under his spell not able to think rationally.

"Mia...Mia, sorry but I love the way that sounds when your name rolls off my tongue, we met before each of us knew who the other was. That wasn't our fault like the way we feel, I want you and you want me. In time Tyler will understand and accept that. Yes it will be hard at first but I also see how much he loves you and I know if you love someone you want them to be happy. He'll be alright once he see's how happy I can make you." Jayce's blue eyes captivating me making me partial believe his twisted reasoning rendering me silent.

"And by the way, you need to quit smoking or I might just have to stop kissing those delicious lips of yours," he got up from the chair and then leaned into the sofa bent over tenderly whispering into my ear.

Just as I started to blush a shade of an unfamiliar name of red you can only find in a crayola box, Tyler walked back in. I got up from the sofa and headed to the kitchen before he could see my face, "I'm making a snack, you boys need anything?"

"Make me and Jayce some sandwiches please ma. We're starving." Tyler said patting his hand down onto his stomach.

"Okay, I gotcha."

"Hey, I'm Beth, I'm Mia's best friend," Her squealing voice caused me to turn around while I walked towards the doors. And there she was, introducing herself to Jayce shaking his hand with raised brows standing in my living room. If the front door wasn't locked she had no issues with making her way in without knocking. Ignoring her calls and texts did me no good knowing that Jayce was here and it was still broad daylight only being two in the afternoon. I guess that gave her an inexcusable reason to show up spontaneously.

"I'm Jayce, nice to meet a friend of Mia's," he politely replied extending a hand out to my soon to be ex nosy best friend.

"Oh you are so adorable," she gushed bringing her hand up to her mouth.

"Beth! Come in here and help me make some sandwiches for the boys. Growing men can eat a lot and I don't think I can make enough sandwiches fast enough to satisfy their hunger," I asserted trying to get her away from Jayce.

Quickly she responded rushing into the kitchen. She waited to say something until we heard the boys making their way up the steps."Oh my God girl, I would totally hit that!" She glowed like she was having an orgasm from just the sight of him.

Seriously? Who are you, Justin Bieber? Who says that?"

"Really girl? He is so fine, you know that don't you? You're both grown adults and Tyler shouldn't affect your relationship."

I got up and poured us a glass of wine. She took her usual seat at the dining room table and I took mine which was our usual ritual when she came over.

"If you had children of your own you'd understand, hurting Tyler like that is a pain worse than death." I told her and meant it, the thought of something more excruciating was inconceivable. Beth had many husbands but no children. Birth control and short marriages played a huge part. She had no idea what is was like to be a parent and love someone so much you were willing to die for them.

"Mom, we're setting up the game in the living room since it's the big screen. You cool with that or do you need to watch your porn in hd?" Tyler peered into the kitchen smirking at his own humor. I hadn't realized he had come back down but luckily he hadn't heard what we were talking about.

"My little boy has grown so much, love you baby. You play your game and not with yourself tonight. My hair conditioner is running low." Again that sibling relationship shined over top of mother and son.

The bound we had was sick and twisted but we shared a love that was stronger than you could find in a storybook. I wanted to find love but deep down I knew I had already found the true meaning. You didn't need a significant other to show you what that meant. Having him was all I needed to be a better person and die content.

"You're such a bitch," he steamed. I could see I had embarrassed him in front of Jayce who hovered behind him not realizing that Tyler wasn't that comfortable around Jayce yet.

Beth quickly saved me, "Tyler you're friend Jayce is hot, is he single?"

Thank you Beth.

"Don't they hold a time span on how many husbands you can have per year? And don't you want to make sure that last divorce is finalized before committing adultery? You could lose your fourth alimony check and you wouldn't want that would you?" Tyler retorted making me proud.

"Such a witty young man, your mom's taught you well," then Beth took a sip of her wine in defeat.

Tyler didn't respond changing his gaze to me. "Mom, me and Jayce are having company tonight. Ashley and Gina are coming over so I need you to stay upstairs."

What? I think the jealously was inadvertently coursing through my veins that second.

CHAPTER 4

B eth helped me make the boys some sandwiches and stuck around for an hour or so longer harassing me the whole time on the Pros of why I should continue my illicit affair until I kicked her out. That woman could be somewhat of a handful at times, okay most of the time, but I loved her despite her flaws.

I went upstairs so I wouldn't end up witnessing Tyler having some make-out session that would want me to wash my eyes out with bleach. It's just as bad as walking in on your parents as a kid. The picture stays burnt in your memory flashing back from time to time like a recurring nightmare. A horror so frightening it's more disturbing than a Rob Zombie movie. I also didn't want to walk in on Jayce foundling some little slut. Why did the idea of him being with someone other than me bother me so much? I swore to myself that I was leaving whatever it was between us alone but I couldn't seem to get him out of my head. It didn't help that we were currently living under the same roof with him literally sleeping feet away from me every night. I wasn't sure if I was keeping my doors locked when everyone went off to bed to keep him out, or to keep me from doing something I would regret.

I decided I would spend my time in lock up buried in online books. I wasn't much in the mood for watching television since everything I use to watch quickly began to bore me after a few episodes and I had seen every movie made in the last twenty years. I walked over to my stereo hooking up my phone and opened up my Spotify account. I put my favorite playlist of trance music on turning up the volume loud enough to drown out any unwanted sounds that would come from downstairs and plopped down on my bed. My back sat up against my headboard with some pillows in between propping me up comfortably with my knees halfway bent up and my feet flat on the mattress.

Now that I had gotten into my reading position I reached over to the side of my bed opening up my night stand drawer to grab my tablet. When I picked it up an old photo of me and Daniel came sliding out of the back. I hadn't used my tablet in two weeks forgetting that I had put that picture in there. I thought we looked so perfect together in the photo, me smiling while he planted a kiss on my cheek. Now I wanted to stab his face out with a pen looking down at him. My eyes began to water, I felt the tears starting to build up trailing down my cheeks. Before I knew it I was in full blown waterfall mode with my eyes swelling to where I could barely open them from all the puffiness. I balled up in my bed holding my knees up against my chest whimpering with my head hung down in between.

I wallowed in my sorrows feeling that piercing pain shoot through my heart yet again from that asshole. I picked up my tablet and flung it across the room shattering it against the wall with a loud thud without thinking it through. I was just so angry and hurt I wanted to break something.

"Is everything okay up there?" Jayce yelled out from the living room.

Shit! I was so tangled up in my grief and anguish I forgot I wasn't the only one in the house. Great, that was the last thing I needed was to ruin Tyler's little date and to have Jayce see me like this.

I tried composing myself so I could give a convincing response before someone came upstairs but it was too late. I couldn't seem to pull myself together and then the knock came rapping on bedroom door.

"Mia let me in, are you alright in there?" Jayces deep voice blared through in worry.

"I'm fine Jayce, don't worry about me," I sniffled uncontrollably not able to hide my sobbing wails.

I could hear the knob handle starting to twist with the door opening behind it. Damn it, I didn't lock my door. I didn't think there was a need with the boys preoccupied with company. Jayce walked in with a concerned look coming in close to me until he took a seat on my bed wrapping his arm around my shoulder.

I fell into him with my head burrowed into his chest soaking his black t-shirt with my tears.

"I'm sorry, it just hurts so much," I cried feeling some comfort as he embraced my body. Somehow he held some warmth I needed to feel so badly.

"It's that Daniel guy isn't it that's got you so upset?" If I ever see him I'll pulverize the dickhead!" Jayce began to steam up in anger as I felt him tense up underneath me.

"He is a dickhead and I'm better off without him. I j..just, I j..ust need some time to move past this," my words stuttered in between my whimpering. "I found an old picture that brought back some bad memories."

"You're too good for a guy like that Mia. Someone as beautiful and amazing as you shouldn't be wasting your tears on such a jerk," and then Jayce put his fingers under my chin lifting my face to his swiping away my tears.

The drops subsided as our eyes met in silence. I don't know how it happened but we were having a moment. He took his finger and trailed it across my bottom lip slightly parting them open. The thought of Daniel quickly diminished as I could feel myself slowly beginning to melt inside from his touch, the shooting waves of electricity sending out sparks.

"You are strikingly attractive, you know that right?" Jayce took his other hand and brushed the loose strands of hair that fell across my face behind my ear causing my body to shudder.

"Y..you, you should go back downstairs to your date and where is Tyler? I would think he would have come upstairs the moment I made all that noise." I was starting to get nervous, first with the concern of Tyler catching us and second because I was about to admit I was starting to have feelings for him.

"Tyler and Ashley left to take Gina home. I was a little too obvious with my disinterest in her company so she got bored and wanted to leave. I don't want a girl, I want a woman, I want you and only you," seriousness rang through his voice and he then leaned in placing a gentle peck on my lips.

How could he possibly be interested in me when he had young beautiful women throwing themselves at his feet? He was too good to be true and he was my son's best friend. "You should go back downstairs. I'm sure Tyler will be back soon and start wondering where you disappeared to." Get rid of him fast, that's what I needed to do.

"Doubtful, him and Ashley seemed liked they wanted some alone time if you know what I mean. I don't think he'll be back home until tomorrow morning at the earliest. Don't worry, I made sure he had condoms with him," and then that evil smirk began to form on his face.

I elbowed Jayce in the stomach for that one.

"Damn, that hurt!" he said still smiling.

"Unfortunately I do know what you mean. You could try to be more discreet. I know Tyler has sex but I still try to pretend in my head he's still a virgin and will stay that way forever," I grimaced cracking a smile.

"Much better, I don't like seeing you cry." Mentioning condoms and my son in the same sentence was cringe worthy but Jayce's descriptive remark did seem to break me away from my depression.

"I'm going to take a shower and you're going to go back downstairs and play videos games," I tried breaking out of his arms but he stiffened his hold not letting me get up.

"I'm only letting you take a shower if I can come join you," he grinned pulling me in even more tighter than before.

I moved into his mouth and licked across his top lip and then sucked repeating myself onto his bottom lip parting his mouth open bringing in my tongue. He started leafing his fingers through my hair pulling our mouths in closer. As soon as I felt his grip loosen on me I sprang up and made a beeline for the bathroom locking the door.

"That was fucked up," Jayce yelled out chuckling.

"Call of Duty, Jayce. Call of Duty," I replied giggling before I stripped down and turned on the water.

My phone started chiming with a text message as I lay in my bed watching Netflix since I had broke my tablet and hated reading off my laptop. Modern technology had spoiled me by just being able to turn a page with a swipe.

Tyler: Spending the night over Ashley's. Be home tomorrow afternoon. Love you

Me: Love you too

Jayce was right, Tyler wasn't coming home until tomorrow which meant I was going to be left alone with him all night. Fuck, I wasn't coming out of my bedroom even if that meant starving myself. Good thing I had my own bathroom with my tiny ass bladder.

Ironically I was forty five minutes into the movie Prime with Uma Thurman and Bryan Greenberg where she was like fifteen years older than him. That relationship tanked in the end, maybe I should take that as a sign. Okay so I had seen it before rewatching it to try to justify being with a much younger man. Their relationship deteriorated because she was ready to settle down and have a family soon where he really wasn't. I already did the family thing and had the kid so me and Jayce were good right? Who was I fooling?

"Open up Mia. You've been hiding in there for the last four hours and you haven't ate since early this morning. I've got pizza and a movie, I know you've got to be starved," Jayce temptingly called through the door while I smelled the aroma of the pizza seeping under the cracks. My mouth started to drool. He was right I was hungry and my stomach was growling at me screaming for me to open up. I started to wonder if I bribed a pizza guy with a large enough tip I could get him to deliver to my bedroom door. Nope that wasn't going to happen, if I tried calling that in they would probably think I was some crazy sheltered cat lady.

"Fine, but only because that pizza smells good as shit," I told him letting him in my room. "Mmm, what kind did you get?" I hunched down inhaling the top of the box.

"Just cheese, I didn't know what you liked and didn't like to eat, besides me of course," Jayce batted his eyes at me.

"You're funny you cocky jerk," I joked furrowing my brows. I like everything except anchovies. Oh, and I hate pineapples on pizza," cringing my face in in disgust.

"Duly noted for next time beautiful," he smiled sitting the pizza down on my bed and then walked over to the dvd player putting the movie in.

"Next time?" I retorted with attitude like that was never going to happen.

Jayce turned around looking up at me from his crouched position in front of the tv pushing the dvd in with a smile slightly laughing, "Don't start or I'm going to have to spank you later."

I just smiled back blushing and then my stomach growled out loud, so embarrassing.

"I knew you were hungry," Jayce chuckled coming back over to the bed taking a seat in front of me. He opened up the box of pizza and grabbed a slice bringing it to my mouth.

"Bite," he commended. I listened without objection. Damn that tasted so good. It was kind of sexy the way he fed me which he kept doing until I finished the slice.

We finished up eating and then Jayce placed the rest of the pizza on my dresser before he came back over besides me on the bed. He lay down cradling me in his grips and pushed play on the remote. I dissolved in his arms resting my head in chest with one arm sprawled out across his waist. He also had one arm around my waist sliding his hand up the bottom of my shirt rubbing up and down with his fingers on the flesh of my lower stomach. We stayed like that through the entire movie reveling in each other's embrace.

When the final credits started to roll Jayce slid his fingers across my jaw bringing my head up to face him. He passionately started kissing me cupping the side of my cheek. I could feel my skin burning up all over kissing him felt so right. How could something that felt so good be so wrong?

"I really like you Jayce," I finally admitted once our swollen lips seperated.

"I really like you too Mia," he started raking his fingers through my hair. My eyes closed and my head fell back down onto his chest taking comfort in his touch and his words as I drifted off asleep.

I woke up in the middle of the night with Jayce spooning me from behind with his arm spread across my mid section and his leg over top of mine locking me underneath him. I pulled his arm in closer to me holding onto it and went back to sleep. I never wanted to let him go.

"Oh Shit! Jayce get up!" and then I shoved his body knocking him off the bed onto the floor freaking out because it was noises from downstairs that had awoken me. We must have overslept because daylight was already shining brightly through the window.

"Damn woman," Jayce said trying to sit up from the floor rubbing his head struggling to open is eyes he was still half asleep.

"Sorry," I looked down at him hanging over the edge of the mattress with a high pitched voice making an apologetic face. I didn't realize I had pushed him so hard. "I 'm sure I just heard the front door slam shut. You need to get out of my room like now!" I panicked.

"Oh shit!" Jayce picked himself up and ran through our joining doors shutting it behind him in a hurry.

"Hey mom," Tyler announced walking through my bedroom door only seconds later.

"Hey baby," I nervously replied still shaken up.

Then Tyler's eyes caught hold of something on the floor with a peculiar look lined across his face. "Why is Jayce's shirt on your floor?" Tyler's voice deepened staring down at the foot of my bed with a look of death in his eyes ready to kill someone.

CHAPTER 5

"What is it with men and leaving their clothes lying around all over the place anyways?" I let out a deep exhale walking over to the edge of my bed picking up the blue polo from the floor. " I found it on the couch yesterday and thought it was yours. I threw it on top of my bed and must have knocked it over forgetting about it. I was going to put it in with the wash," I vented in frustration and then turned my head raising it to face Jayce's room.

"I hope you heard that Jayce! You guys need to stop throwing your crap all over the house," I yelled out like I was aggravated.

When I turned back to Tyler walking towards the hamper, he had a dumbfounded look on his face to my relief. I got myself out of what could have been a disaster but the knot balled up in my stomach told me this wasn't going to be the last time I was going to have to bullshit my way out a sticky situation.

"Sorry Mia, won't happen again," Jayce replied back through the wall.

I felt fear, guilt, and confusion all together at that moment. How was I going to let this continue knowing that eventually the truth was going to find a way of coming out and then all hell was going to break loose? I was going to have to have one serious talk with Jayce later when Tyler wasn't around.

"Sorry mom, for a second I thought...." and then he paused not continuing his statement, "you know what? It was nothing," Tyler nodded it off. "I'm going to go take a nap, Ashley had me up all night," and then a large smirk laced across his face. Tyler obviously had his suspicions but nothing had been confirmed. I was really pushing my luck yet dodging another close call.

"TMI, TMI!" I bellowed out with my eyes shut and my hands over my ears nodding my head in denial.

Tyler just laughed leaning in and giving me a peck on the cheek before he finally left my room and went off to his bedroom.

That was it, things were ending right now with me and Jayce. I didn't know how much longer I could endure these close encounters on top of all these mixed emotions.

I waited at least twenty minutes until Tyler had left before I would go over to talk to Jayce. I wanted to make sure Tyler was in bed sleeping or at least in his bed relaxed to where he wasn't going to get up anytime soon. I locked my bedroom door and walked over to the adjoining door that divided us.

I didn't knock just barging in with authority ready to put my foot down, "Ja....," I fell into a catatonic state unprepared to find him standing there wrapped only in a towel with pellets of water trickling down his broad chest. The speech I had lined up in my head completely disappeared. They were replaced by the thoughts of removing that towel and licking him from top to bottom. I felt myself trembling remembering how his touch could send earth quaking tremors throughout my body bringing me to a state of euphoria.

"You wanted to say something Mia?' he looked up shaking off the excess water from his hair giving me that wicked grin of his that could cause nuns to break their oath of celibacy.

"I..I..I can't talk to you when you're like this," I quickly threw my hands up covering my eyes. "Put some clothes on," I demanded, blood rushing to my face.

"Nope," he chuckled and then I could feel his body heat radiating, Jayce moving in closer until I could feel his breath touching the back of my neck. Oh God, I was going to need to start going to confession after this.

I heard his towel drop to the floor and then his fingers gently swiped the back of my hair to one side of my head exposing my neckline. His lips moved in trailing his tongue below my ear licking and kissing. The shivering sensations swept through my body awakening that painful ache that yearned for relief.

He took me in devouring my most sensitive areas at the back of my neck just above my shoulder. Each time his lips met my flesh my entirety shuddered anxiously anticipating his moist mouth sampling my taste.

I bit down hard on my bottom lip trying to contain my moans unsuccessfully.

"You were saying something Mia?" Jayce whispered and then returned back to seductively torturing me.

"Jayce..this..this has to stop," slowly came out of my mouth between my hitching breath.

"Whatever you say," he mocked me bringing his hands around my waist up to my breasts flicking my nipples with his fingers underneath my nightshirt. His mouth still taking advantage of me from behind while I felt his hard cock pressing up against my back.

"If that's what you really want I'll stop right now. Tell me, is that what you want?" His hands and mouth paused in a stand still awaiting a reply.

"Give me a minute to think this through," I panted taking one of his hands down between my legs. I proceeded to guide his fingers underneath mine rubbing the wet crease inside my panties. Back and forth I led his fingers assisting him in heightening my stimulation, both our hands soon lay drenched down below.

I let my other hand take his other massaging my breast together. I found it exceedingly pleasing playing with myself over top of him.

"I'm going to be rough with you now and you're going to like it. Are you okay with that?" Jayce's voice grew more stern and then he took a hard bite into my shoulder. I let out a loud shrill caught off guard. It hurt but the pain quickly disintegrated turning into desperate anticipation. It was a physical infliction that left me needing more.

Thankfully Tyler's room was in the basement, he would have definitely heard me if he were upstairs.

"Yes, I want you to punish me. I've been a naughty girl."

"Good, that's what I want to hear," I could feel the content ring through his voice and then he turned me around crashing his lips against mine. Adamantly he kissed me before taking grasps of my shoulders shoving me down to my knees.

"Open your mouth for me baby.

I complied.

He stroked his manhood several times before smacking my bottom lip with his pre-cumming tip. "Do you want this?"

"Yes. I want to make you feel good." His teasing member was so inviting it was making me plead to relish it in my mouth.

"Then I want to hear you beg saying my name," he was being so forceful and dominating turning me on as he flicked himself on my bottom lip once again.

"Please Jayce. I wanna fuck you with my mouth," I begged looking up into his eyes with lust.

"Good girl," then he shoved his hard cock down my throat holding my head and I instantly I reached up and started stroking at the same time still sucking. Mmm he was so delicious. He pumped his dick in and out so far I could feel him touching my tonsils forcing me to gag several times.

I looked up keeping my eyes wide open meeting his gaze watching him taking pleasure in my mouth, Jayce moaning and panting enjoying every second. I didn't care how much his size made me choke, I just kept going taking him in all the way down. I didn't want him to finish desperate to feel him inside. I would stop sucking bringing my tongue to the bottom of his shaft licking up to his head while I still stroked. I'd twirl my tongue around his tip tasting his salty pre-juices bringing my lips back down for small strides with my tongue lacing his member.

"Okay Mia I want you to get up and take off all your clothes. Do you want me to fuck you now?," he yanked my hair back pulling my head away so he could meet my eyes directly with his own.

"Yes," I looked at him my eyes beseeching with the empty space between my legs twitching to feel his thick firmness. The rest if my clothes came off after that.

"Yes what?" he bitterly asserted grabbing my neck in between his fingers only leaving me with a just enough air to breath in and out to function. I couldn't complain, the tightness of his grip and shortness of my breath increased my gratification pushing me closer to my goals.

"Please Jayce, I need you to fuck me," I yearned in desperation.

"Much better. Get up against the wall and turn around."

I did as I was told hearing Jayce opening a drawer with the sounds of crinkling plastic being ripped open following shortly after. I stood there shivering impatiently while he approached from behind grabbing my arms and throwing them up above my head flattening my hands against the wall.

He placed one hand on top of mine with his free hand guiding his stiff long shaft into my passageway hammering with a hard thrust. My body flung up hard against the wall Jayce shoved into me with such force causing me to let out a loud surprised groan. He pumped himself in me back in forth with anger fondling my nub with his fingers.

"Ohmygod, ohmygod, ohmygod," I panted aloud unable to mask the intense pleasure that had me all shaken up.

He plowed and thrashed so fast I could feel his large hardness in the pits of my stomach. He continued to push into me so violently it hurt but at the same time felt amazing outweighing the pain.

My eyes rolled back behind my head as I reached my climax releasing a boisterous squeal of contempt. Jayce continued to thrust in madness bringing me back to that point two more times until he yelled out in his own release. His body fell limp and weak twisting me around to face him.

"Did you like that?" he asked with a smile nibbling on my lips.

"Well I came three times so what do you think?" I asked sarcastically with a smirk just before I started raking my fingers through his hair kissing him passionately.

Jayce just smiled back reciprocating my firy kisses.

After we finished making out he removed the condom throwing it in the waste basket and then threw on a pair of boxers before sprawling out comfortably on his bed.

"Lay with me for a little while Mia," Jayce patted his hand down on the mattress trying to cajole me by his side.

"I should get back to my room now," I gathered my scattered garments quickly placing my panties back on and then slipped my head underneath my shirt.

"Mia if you don't get in this bed with me right now I swear I'll scream so loud Tyler will wake up and come up stairs," He threatened laying back relaxed on his mattress with the utmost confidence. "You don't want me tell him how naughty his mommy really is do you?"

"You wouldn't?!" I whipped my head around in fear to face him as I was making my way to our adjoining doors to get to my bedroom.

"No, I think Tyler could kick my ass and he would if he knew what I just did you to you but I don't want you to go yet. Please just come over here for a little while. You're always running away from me." I could see the desperation in his eyes with sincerity ringing through his tone, how could I deny him?

"Fine," I willingly agreed but it wasn't a hard decision to make, I wanted to. There was that angel on my shoulder with his white dress and halo that sat there consistently telling me to walk away but then there was that little devil on the other side pitchfork in hand that had me flicking that angel off letting my hormones control my better judgement. Red pitchfork guy seemed to win every time hands down.

My body fell down besides him wrapping my arms around his torso looking up meeting his gaze. I stared at him silently not making any advances with my lips locked in a closed smile and a twinkling spark in my eyes.

"Why are you looking at me like that?" Jayce raised a brow with a look of bewilderment.

"No reason," I lied but I knew exactly why. When I got involved with Daniel a part of me died, I use to feel alive like I could conquer the world and nothing could get me down but I lost that when we were together. I always sensed that part of me was missing not knowing how to get it back. I realize now that my subconscious was telling me all along that Daniel didn't belong in my life. Since that first night with Jayce I've started to feel like myself again, strong, fearless, like there's no storm I can't weather and I know he gave that back to me.

Jayce cupped my jawline tenderly running his fingers towards my chin raising my face to meet his.

"You're glowing right now, did you know that? I don't think it was the sex that is making you this way either. I didn't think you could get anymore beautiful but apparently you've proved me wrong."

My eyes lowered as my cheeks fell flush In embarrassment not knowing what to say from his sweet words. He always seemed to have a way of making me blush at the same time making feel special.

"I want you to hang out with me and Tyler tonight. We talked about having a poker game later with a couple more friends."

What?! Well that just killed the moment as my head sprung up and my eyes bulged out like saucers looking at him like he was insane.

"What? Are you fucking crazy???"

Chapter 6

"Tyler's told me how you use to just hang out with him and his friends every once in awhile just to have some quality time with him. He said that all changed, you changed, once you started dating Daniel and it wasn't for the better. This way you can spend time with Tyler and we can do something together. Beside's, I heard you can get pretty entertaining when you get drunk. Not that I don't find you entertaining already, you always keep me interested," and then he started laughing.

I had done some really embarrassing things when I was drunk around Tyler and his friends. God only knows what humiliating stories were shared with Jayce. I had been so wasted one night it took me two days to remember Tyler had convinced me to have a free styling rap battle against his friend Bran. Luckily everyone was so drunk that night no one realized to videotape the whole embarrassing ordeal. That would have definitely found it's way to YouTube.

"Okay, first of all I don't even want to know what they've told you and second of all, No. I was right, you are crazy." He just chuckled some more.

"Please," he begged placing butterflies kisses down the nape of my neck.

"Hmmm, ...still noooo," hesitantly the words came out of my mouth moaning simultaneously leaning my head back with my lids shut basking in his caress melting like butter.

"If you don't then I'm forcing you to go on a date with me tomorrow and I'm not taking no for an answer. So what's it going to be gorgeous?"The kisses had stopped and Jayce had shifted his eyes up looking at me with an ice cold stare. I knew he was serious and as much I wished I could say yes there was no way I was taking the chance of being seen in public with him alone.

"What are you going to do? Fly us two states over on your private jet to some remote location where nobody knows us?" I said deadpanned getting up from the bed.

Jayce reached out taking my arm before I could escape back to my room, "Mia seriously, we're not going to be able to keep sneaking around forever and I want to do something with you. This isn't just some fling for me." I knew he cared and I wasn't just a lay to him but fuck me, a rubix cube was less complicated then this whole mess.

"Fine, you win. I'll play poker with you guys tonight but I need to get back to my room now. I've been in here long enough already," I turned back to Jayce hunching over giving a him a kiss before I walked off taking my arm back. His kisses were so addictive always suckling at my lips first before our tongues would entwine. I needed one last one not knowing when the next time would be.

"It's a date then," I didn't have to see it to know he was smiling cheek to cheek from the content in his tone when he yelled that out before I closed the door behind me.

I had run out to the gas station and grabbed a pack of cigarettes before tonight's festivities took place. I couldn't hold back the urge to chain smoke today stressed about how tonight was going to pan out. When alcohol played a part I was hornier than a dog in heat and having Jayce in the same room as me all night not being able to feel his sensual touch or divine kisses was going to having me sparking up like fireworks on the Fourth of July. I must suffer from one of those sexual addictions because I constantly craved sex twenty four seven and drinking only made it worst. Unlike most women I hit my sexual peak before my teens and never grew out of it.

Now that Beth had finally met Jayce I felt a little bit more at ease with her being in the same room as the two of us inviting her over for tonight. I knew she would probably embarrass me but I was feeling more comfortable that she wasn't going to give up my secret. I also needed someone to watch over me in case I started getting out of hand.

"Hey Beth, the boys are having a little poker game tonight and I need you to be my wingman and make sure I don't do anything stupid," I told her through my bluetooth system driving back from the Shell station.

"Is Bran going to be there?!" You could already hear her excitement ringing through the line. A lot of Tyler's friends were quite attractive young men but Beth was obsessed with Bran never making it a secret that she was fond of him. He stood just under 6 feet with golden blond hair and a sculpted body just like the rest of the boys. Bran always played along flirting back but never took Beth seriously. He had too many young attractive women vying for his attention to be concerned with an older woman's crush.

"Yea, we can be the Milf squad. You and Bran, me and Jayce," I joked even though technically she wasn't a mother.

"Just give me a time and I'll be there with the White Zinfandel."

"I think they said they were starting around 8:00 but if you want to get here earlier I don't mind hitting up a couple of glasses beforehand to calm my nerves," My hormones didn't need the extra push but I could use something to loosen me up because I was freaking the fuck out already three cigarettes in.

"Chill out chicka, I'll get showered and ready now. I can get there in forty minutes and we'll have over an hour to get our buzz on. And then later I can get my groove on like Stella," she chuckled.

"Just remember Stella's man ended up being gay in real life," I teased.

"I haven't even started drinking yet and you're already a buzz kill. I'll see you soon," she grimaced.

"By Beth," and then I hung up the phone.

I pulled up to the house with Tyler, Jayce, Bran, and Adam one of their other buddies standing out front playing around wrestling in the yard with beers already in hand. Tyler and Bran were on the grass rolling around going body flaunting their male testosterone.

"Umps, umps, umps, umps," Jayce came up to my car bobbing his head vigorously crossing his arms in and out making waves mocking my trance music I had blaring from my speakers.

"Are you making fun of my music?" I scowled with a grin cutting off the engine getting out of the car.

"Never, I love this stuff. I can even twerk to it see," and then he turned around shaking his ass with his front hands clasped together mocking me even more. Everyone including me burst out in laughter he looked so ridiculous. Good thing I didn't meet him at a club or I would have never gone home with him after witnessing that eyesore of a sight.

"You like my dancing skills don't you?" Jayce smirked winking at me.

Bam! and there it came. Tyler came up from behind tackling Jayce down to the ground with a hard thud.

"Stop flirting with my mom," Tyler asserted in a deep tone hovered over Jayce with Jayce still facing the dirt lifting himself up off of the ground. Tyler's face proudly donned a cryptic smirk of content looking down at Jayce before facing me with that same evil smile.

"You know sometimes you can be a real ass Tyler," I shrugged my shoulders nodding my head with a frown disturbed by his actions.

"Shit Jayce, your legs all scraped up!," I had redirected my glance back to Jayce who was now standing with blood trailing down his shin.

"Oh come on mom, Jayce knows I was just playing." His voice was so empty lacking emotion it scared me. It was like he was nonchalantly trying to get his point across reminding Jayce that he was bigger and stronger and not to be fucked with especially when it came to me.

"Mia I'm fine," Jayce tried shaking it off never looking back at Tyler. I think he knew there was already too much tension now between the two of them and decided to leave things alone to my relief. Tyler wasn't stupid, he could sense the attraction between me and Jayce even though he didn't know the details. Tyler was making it known that he knew something and he definitely didn't approve. Everybody else just stood back silently in shock.

I looked back at Tyler fuming in rage, " All of a sudden you're going psycho because Jayce and me actually get along? I think sometimes you forget I had you when I was young and I'm not that much older than most of your buddies so we're going to able to relate. I can't change the fact that I'm not like your friends mothers who are all in their fifties. I got pregnant when I was I a kid and I'm not sorry about that because I have you now."

I had dated men as young as Jayce before and it had never bothered Tyler. My parents were fourteen years apart and had been happily married for twenty five years proving age could sometimes only be a number. It was only because Jayce was Tyler's friend that he was acting this way but if they hadn't known each other Tyler wouldn't give a shit if he knew we were dating as long as Jayce wasn't some abusive douche.

Since Jayce came into my life being with him made me feel emotions and sensations I never knew existed in me. My pulse raced and my heart would pound so hard it felt like it could burst out of my chest whenever I was around him. I couldn't give that up, I wouldn't give that up but what was I going to do about Tyler??

"Whatever," Tyler dismissed me walking back over to his group of friends.

"Come on Jayce, I'm going to get you cleaned up. You're dripping blood all over." His leg was pretty battered. I could see a significantly large gash just below his knee that needed to be taken care of.

"It's just a scratch, I'll be okay," Jayce tried to pretend like it wasn't bothering him but I could see in his face he was struggling to hold back from showing any pain.

"Don't argue with me!" I defiantly declared. The mother in me was dominating and not taking no for an answer which he quickly caught on to following behind me into the house.

I led us to my bedroom because my bathroom had all the antiseptics and bandages and I commanded him to take a seat on my bed.

Mia, I....."

"Shut up and sit there while I get something to take care of that cut," I interrupted. Whatever he was about to say held no ground at the moment. He was hurt and I wasn't falling for the tough guy act.

I went to bathroom and gathered some peroxide, cotton balls and band aids making my way to the edge of the bed in front of Jayce kneeling down to patch him up.

Jayce just looked down on me in silence as I poured some peroxide on a cotton ball taking it to his leg cleansing his wound. Gently I patted the cut until all the blood was removed and then I lightly blew on it to dry up his skin so I could place a band aid on.

"Okay, which one do you want? I've got Spongebob or Dora band aids." I asked with a monotone voice.

"In light of everything that just happened you can still make jokes. It things like that that makes me so attracted to you," Jayce chuckled.

"No seriously, Spongebob or Dora? I couldn't help it okay, they were just so cute I had to buy them," I whimpered in embarrassment turning my head not wanting him to see my reddening face.

I was a sex craved, immature thirty five year old woman. There was something seriously wrong with me.

"You're so adorable, you know you look like a hot grown Dora?" Jayce playfully insinuated displaying that addictive smile of his.

"Keep it up and I'll pour alcohol over your leg instead of perox-ide," I threatened meeting his hypnotic eyes but didn't succumb to his appeal.

Jayce just leaned his head back laughing in amusement.

"Alright, you're getting Dora bitch," and then I placed the girly band aid on his leg having to use three of them to cover his thick muscular shin but then I hung my head down and started to tear up.

"Hey, what's wrong? Why are you crying beautiful?" Jayce reached down lifting me up placing me besides him on the bed taking my hand into his. Worried eyes fell into mine with concern.

"I don't want to give up what I feel when I'm with you but I don't want to destroy my son either. You make me smile and laugh, it's always so easy to talk to you. I'm comfortable around you and feel so at ease putting me at loss right now. How would you feel if you thought one of your friends had something going on with your mother?" the moist drops continued to flow down my cheeks.

"I'd feel pity on my friend. My mother cheated and stole half of my dad's money besides getting pregnant by another man while she was still married. When her boyfriend saw her for who she really was he didn't want anything to do with my mom or sister. Mom split and left Andrea with me and my dad. Even though she wasn't his flesh and blood he learned to love her for my sake because she was my little sister and because my father's a good man." I could hear his hurt making me fall weak.

"I'm so sorry, I didn't know."

"How could you? It's okay," he said leafing my hair back with one hand and swiping away my tears with the other. "Everything's going to fine, you forget I know how Tyler is too. He's hot headed but eventually he'll cool off and understand when you're ready to tell him." That was the problem, Tyler was headstrong and I was starting to come to the conclusion that he would never give his approval no matter who's side was right or wrong. And poor Jayce, I had no clue his mother was so fucked up.

I fell into his arms desperate for his comforting warmth and needing for him to know I wasn't going anywhere. I needed to be pulling away but his confession and vulnerability only brought me in closer. He trusted me enough to confide something so dark letting me know for certain what we had was something real, something worth fighting for.

I couldn't contain myself any longer moving our mouths in together until we were one. My swollen lips being conquered by his own quickly diminishing my worries and fears bringing me back into that world where only him and I existed and nothing else mattered.

All of a sudden we were interrupted, I pulled back from his arms in a jolt hearing the bedroom door fling open.

"What the fuck are you two doing?" a voice called out sending shooting waves of fear throughout my body as I looked up towards the doorway.

<h1 style="text-align:center">Chapter 7</h1>

"**D**amn it Beth, you almost gave me a heartache! I think I just peed myself. I thought you were Tyler," I sighed out a deep breath grateful it wasn't my son standing before me. I think I really did almost pee myself I was so petrified when I heard the door burst open. I looked over to Jayce and his face was a sheepish white obviously feeling the same horror I had just felt.

"If it had been Tyler you wouldn't have had time to have a heartache. He would have killed you both before you had a chance to die so easily,"Beth lectured me entering my room shutting the door behind her. I had forgotten she was on her way over I was so preoccupied with Jayce and our fucked up predicament.

"You two need to pull yourselves together and get your asses downstairs asap before Tyler ends up here. There's so much heat in this room right now I feel like I'm the one who needs the cold shower," she started fanning her face with her hand releasing a breath.

"We'll be down in a minute," and then I noticed Beth was holding an opened bottle of wine in her other hand. From time to time we had the tendency to leave out the minor details when it came to our wine like glasses for instance. We would just chug straight from the bottle.

"Oh my god, give me that!," I jumped up from the bed and came at her like I was a predator ready to attack prying the bottle out of her fingers. I brought the bottle to my lips and starting guzzling it down. I needed something to calm my shaken nerves.

"Geeze Mia! Sometimes I forget you can drink like a fish when you want to," she snatched the bottle out of my mouth in mid motion leaving a portion dripping from my lips down to the floor. I hadn't realized in that one gulp I had already taken down half of a 1.5 liter bottle. "I'm going back down and I expect you guys to follow shortly. Oh and by the way, some girl Gina is downstairs looking for you Jayce. I forgot that was the whole reason I came up here," and then Beth turned away leaving making sure she left the door wide open so we didn't do anything else stupid.

Gina, that was the girl that was at the house the other day trying to get with Jayce! My blood started to boil with jealousy. I knew she was going to drape herself all over him in front of me and there was nothing I would be able to do except watch torturously in silence.

"Hello?? Mia? Did you hear anything I just said?" I turned my head back over in Jayce's direction noticing the color had returned back to his face but anything he might have just said a minute ago went completely over my head. I was too distracted by my hatred for a girl I had never even met or seen. She probably looked just like Barbie, all the females Tyler brought home did.

"Hum, what?" I looked at him bewildered with my mouth partial-ly gaped open.

"I said, so Beth knows about us right?"

"Um yeah, she's good. She won't say anything, now let's go down-stairs." I just got up facing the door and walked away leaving Jayce behind. I was starting to feel the wine making it's way through my bloodstream but it was nowhere near enough. I was ready to take down a whole brewery now unable to focus on anything but the thoughts of Gina and her wandering hands. Jayce told me before he held no interest in Gina but it wasn't like he was my boyfriend and after Daniel I had some serious trust issues when it came to a man's sincerity.

I went down to Tyler's room where everybody had already start-ed to get situated sitting at the table drinking with a deck of cards and chips centered in the middle. When I looked over to Tyler he was leaned back in a chair with an attractive brunette perched on his lap who I assumed could only be Ashley. They were both smiling and giggling with her arms wrapped around his neck. Yuck! It was disturbing on so many levels watching your own child show intimacy towards the opposite sex knowing exactly what he was thinking or should I say thinking with. Ewe, double yuck! Then my eyes strayed to the left not able to endure the disturbing visions any longer that were making me want to shove my fingers down my throat.

And there she was, that had to be Gina standing up from a hunch positioned in front of the mini fridge getting a beer. When she fully stood up shutting the door she turned her body with her head wisping her long blonde wavy hair in the air exposing her flawless skin like she was a model shooting a Heineken commercial. I was right, she looked like Mattel had taken one of their Barbies fresh out of the box and given it life. She was gorgeous with her perky breasts and pear shaped figure strutting towards a seat like she just got off the catwalk until she finally got to her chair. I secretly hoped like Barbie she wasn't anatomically correct as I found more of a reason to feel jealous now seeing her. She was perfect in every way I needed to find some flaw even if it was seriously unlikely.

"Oh Jayce, come sit next to me. I saved you a seat," her face garnished a large ecstatic grin gazing at the figure behind me as she patted her hand down on the empty chair gesturing for him to come over.

"Jayce made his way past me not looking back once like I wasn't even there, "Sure, let me grab a drink first."

That hurt. It was Daniel all over except Jayce wasn't even trying to hide it.

"Hey Mia, come take the seat next to me," Adam one of Tyler's other close friends called happily. Adam always seemed to bear a small crush on me but I disregarded it even though he was quite attractive. I knew him from Tyler not a one night stand so the rules with him were different. I first and always saw him as just one of my son's friends. He was twenty four, with golden blonde hair and also frequented the gym like all the others holding a defined build. Tyler was actually the youngest out of everybody but he looked and acted older leading him to hang out with a much more mature group instead of people his own age. All of my son's friends were hot ,legal, and off hands. Yeah me! Not that any of that mattered anymore if somehow I was allowed to see them in a different light. Jayce was the only one I wanted.

"Thanks Adam, let me grab a beer and I'll be right there," new rules, I had no intention of getting with Adam but I was going to flirt like hell broken from Jayce's blatant disregard to my existence and full awareness of Gina's. I had known Adam for years and Tyler knew I had no sexual interest in him so I was going to be able to get away with some playful ogling.

"I'll get it for you!" Adam bostoriously leaped from his seat racing to the fridge. I took the empty seat besides Adam's directly across from Jayce and Gina.

"You're such a sweetheart," I smirked in his direction batting my lashes.

Jayce had taken his seat next to Gina and I made sure I avoided eye contact not wanting him to sense my jealousy and how upset I really was. No matter how hard this was going to be I was making sure I wouldn't let my true emotions be seen.

Immediately Gina started talking to Jayce all smiles touching him every chance she got placing her hand on his shoulder, his thighs, and anywhere else she could physically make contact. Urrgh!! I wanted to jump up across the table and pound my fist into her cheery face. I know it was wrong but for a brief moment I had believed Jayce had cared about me making witnessing this hurt so much more.

Adam had come back over handing me my beer and I took it down in seconds. For some reason bottled beer flowed down my throat smoother than water diminishing in less than a minute.

"Damn Mia, I wouldn't want to go against you in a drinking contest," Adam looked at me in astonishment.

"Oh come on Adam, don't tell me you're scared to go one on one with lil old me? Let's have a little fun before the poker game. Go grab some more beers and whoever finishes last has to guzzle another one," I didn't let my gaze break from Adam flirtatiously pulling him into my allure.

He looked at me with a victorious smile, like he had finally broken some ground after all these years making leeway towards his goals. Little did he know I was just trying to get at Jayce, part of me felt bad for misleading him but another side of me didn't' care only wanting revenge. I can't believe I actually thought he cared about me but he was just like all the guys I had dated before if not worse.

Adam went and got more drinks and we went head to head with me winning the first battle. Of course Adam was no good with being defeated challenging me to another duel. Everyone sat back entertained forgetting about the card game.

Adam won one or two while I did the same sneaking in a shot of rum here and there starting to feel the alcohol take it's full effects. "I love you Adam, you're always so much fun," I bellowed out taking my arms around his neck and placing a large moist kiss on the side of his face. Tyler ignored my exuberance more preoccupied with Ashley. I was sure if it was Jayce I had been throwing myself at Tyler wouldn't have been so adamant to interrupt my drunken behavior sending me off to my room to sleep it out but Tyler knew, he knew I would never cross that line when it came to Adam.

Jayce had somehow taken notice though right after I observed him whispering in Gina's ear with her face practically glowing when he pulled his lips away from her ears. The claws were slightly starting to protrude from my fingers. No one else seemed to care that I was drunk draping myself all over Adam. Tyler and Ashley were off in there own world while Beth and Bran sat adjacent to me with Beth to distracted indulged in Bran's attention since no other girls were around.

"Tyler," Jayce looked over towards my son," I think your mom's had enough." His voice was stern and serious. "Maybe someone should help her upstairs." Really? He was just whispering sweet nothings to his new toy, now he's trying to get me sent off to bed like I'm the child. The nerve.

"I've got her ,"Adam called out eager to carry me off like a knight in shining armor.

"I want another beer!" I pouted not ready to end my suffering. I was only torturing myself watching Jayce with someone else ignorant to my presence until I was to the point of making a fool out of myself. I couldn't bring myself to leave secretly hoping this was some sick ruse of his and he would come back to me.

Why did he care all of sudden about me anyways?? Did he think I was going to do something outlandish to screw up his chances with Gina? Which I probably would have if Tyler wasn't around but no amount of alcohol or the way I felt about Jayce would drive me that far. That would only confirm Tyler's suspicions.

"Mia go to bed, your wasted," Jayce declared. At the same time Gina edged her seated stance in closer to Jayce taking her hand to his face directing his view to hers. She spoke softly under her breath so no one else could hear but him and then started placing butterfly kisses on the nape of his neck. I couldn't comprehend his reaction only seeing a blur I had drank so much. The only thing I knew was that I felt an overpowering hatred for the both of them and I wanted another drink.

"Sharing is caring!" I screamed out pulling up from my seat. When I got to my feet I quickly lost my composure almost stumbling to the ground but recollected myself in time before I literally busted my ass.

"Mom, maybe Jayce is right. I think you might have had a little too much to drink," Tyler had finally broke away from Ashley's lock on him looking up at me but his words were slurred. It was like he was able to partially rationalize momentarily in his drunken state.

"The boys are right, you've hit your limit. Go get some rest," Beth added in.

I ignored her looking back toward Jayce who's attention was focused back on Gina. She was now sitting comfortably on his lap brushing her breasts up against his shoulder. Skank!

"Just wait and see, I'm going to Carebear stare on all you moth-erkfuckers and then you'll feel my wrath!," I ranted now wobbling on my feet. Witnessing Gina and Jayce almost ready to take it the next level had me livid. Yes I was drunk but I was also in pain and angry not able to restrain the emotions that were building up in me for much longer. Maybe I should just go to bed before I did or said something I couldn't take back. Thank you god, some sanity was starting to makes its way to my brain holding me back from getting too out of line.

"I've got you," I looked over and Adam was entwining our arms together leading me towards the steps. Vagina! I yelled in my head as I sneered. I don't know why, maybe it was my perverse personality but somehow that was always the word that I wanted to scream, that or fuck if not both, when I was frustrated. It hadn't been clinically diagnosed but it seemed to be more than obvious I had some kind of chemical imbalance.

When we got to my room all I wanted to do was jump onto my bed and crash, forget what my eyes had witnessed almost bringing me to tears. I faltered making my way to my bed forgetting Adam was right behind me and started lifting off my t-shirt over my head leaving only my bra and buttoned cotton shorts exposed.

Adam moved into me without notice and pulled me into his lips which I unconsciously gave into. For a second I thought he was Jayce wanting so badly to feel his touch. When Adam's tongue twirled with mine I quickly realized it wasn't Jayce I was kissing. With Jayce his kisses were always so delicate but demanding. When any part of our bodies met I found myself feeling an intense sensation that stung my insides awaking something dormant and I wasn't feeling that knowing it couldn't be him.

My eyes widened seeing it was Adam meeting my lips swiftly jerking back breaking away.

"Adam I'm sorry I misled you. I'm really drunk and horny. I can't be anything but Tyler's mom when it comes to you. I love you and always will but in a motherly way. I hope you can forgive me," I covered my revealing upper torso with my arms crossed in embarrassment.

Are you sure about that? I was getting a vibe that told me you liked it when I kissed you," Adam stood there in confidence clueless that my heart already belonged to someone else.

"If I had met you under any other circumstances this might have worked but this isn't going to happen," I assured him narrowing my face with certainty.

"Goodnight Mia," the poor thing looked liked a lost puppy dog as he moved back turning around walking out.

I felt horrible but I was glad he was gone. I loved Adam but could never be in love with him. As soon as he walked out I dropped down onto the bed passing out.

I could feel a moist wet tongue making it's way up my inner thigh causing me to shiver in my bed. I had to be dreaming but if I was then please don't wake me up because it felt so fucking good! I lay there embracing my fantasy imagining it was Jayce gradually trailing his lips up towards my fold.

"Please don't stop,"my voice quivered with my fingers clutching onto my sheets in an excited restraint waiting to be devoured in between.

"I'm not going to stop baby, I love the way your juices flow read for me to taste them," the voice in my head sounded like Jayce's leaving me gasping for more of what was to come.

My hips thrusted upwards as his mouth made its way just below my lips calling out the be desecrated.

"Jayce I want you so bad," I moaned.

"Are you sure it's me not Adam you want?" the lips halted.

I opened my eyes in surprise, I wasn't dreaming. My remaining clothing had been removed with only my bra still in tact with Jayce hovered above me looking into my eyes with questionable doubt.

I was still pretty drunk but I was also hurt and pissed,"What the fuck do you think you're doing? Shouldn't you be with your Malibu Barbie right now?" I had sprung up from the bed in seated position fuming causing him to reel back.

"Did you seriously think I was into her? I told you already I only want you. I didn't know she was going to be here but I had to play the part so Tyler and the guys wouldn't think anything and that's what I thought you were doing too with Adam. At least that's what I thought at first but then you looked like you were really getting into him. That's why I sent your ass off to bed." Wow, I could hear the anger and jealousy in his voice, did I really effect him the same way he did me?

"I could say the same for you and you're beach blonde bimbo Barbie. What, you decided you didn't want to play with her anymore tonight so you put her back in her box?" I couldn't help be a bitch still irritated. If he had been playing a part then kudos because he pulled it off a little too well.

"Adam might want to sleep with me but I've watched him grow up from being a bed wetter to a grown man. I love him like a son and would never consciously do something with him." I had to add in that consciously part remembering how I slipped up and let him kiss me but I didn't know what I was doing when it happened.

Jayce just started laughing.

"What? What's so funny?" Where was he finding humor at a time like this?

"Malibu Barbie, beach blonde bimbo Barbie, you'v got a vivid imagination," he chuckled some more, " and Adam use to wet the bed? I can't wait to tease him about that one."

"No you can't!" I screamed out in horror. Adam would be so embarrassed. "Shit, I'm going to wake up Tyler!" I realized how loud I was after I yelled out.

"Tyler is out for the night he was so drunk he passed out before I left the room. Ashley wasn't to happy about that one. And as for Gina, yes, I will admit she is striking but she also has no personality of her own agreeing with anything you say and she's boring as all hell. The only thing she knows how to talk about is her clothes, her hair and her make-up. How could I possibly want someone so clueless over you? You're fun, smart,and fearless never afraid to say or do what you want. You care more about everybody else then yourself always cleaning up after us, fixing our diners, putting Tyler's feelings over top of yours, and your beautiful. Who needs Malibu Barbie when I've got Dora the Explorer anyways?," he added in making me laugh.

"Well you really had me going so now you're going to have to make it up to me," the revelation that Tyler was out for the night and we could be as loud as we want just dawned on me. Maybe the whole Gina thing had been an act but I was still going to punish him for putting me through tonight and we were definitely going to be making some noise.

"Like how?" I had peaked his curiosity.

"You're about to find out."

Chapter 8

As much as I enjoyed being dominated I also needed to have control sometimes and tonight was going to be one of those times I was in charge.

"First of all you're going to finish what you were just doing," I commanded unsnapping my bra tossing it to the ground. Then I leaned back resting my head on my pillow after I switched on my miniature Tiffany lamp on my nightstand. I wanted to make sure he was going to be able to witness everything.

"Oh and don't think about taking off your boxers yet," which was the only thing he was wearing.

"I think I like this already," he enthusiastically obeyed moving his firm hands down to my thighs bringing his face down in between.

I gave him a look of approval while he slid his moist wet tongue up and down my thigh moving to the next then stared up at me real quick to see my reactions before he continued.

I let him trail his tongue around for a little while before meeting my center as I began to gasp heavily becoming impatient to feel him licking my most sensitive of areas.

I ran my fingers through his soft hair pulling it in my fingers shoving his face down in between, "Now lick! and use your fingers, I want to feel you pumping inside of me while your mouth takes me in," I forcefully asserted.

"Mia you are so hot right now," his eyes moved up to meet mine for a moment with a delighted smile.

"Yes, just like that," I moaned aloud when I felt that first lick hit inside the middle of my most plumpest of lips.

His tongue pierced inside me he had somehow moved from licking my cunt to fucking it with his mouth. In and out his tongue striked then he took his fingers pulling my fold open making an upside down V. With his other hand he took two fingers inside me pumping them vigorously with his tongue relocating just above making waves. I was completely revealed at his mercy relishing every second.

"Keep going, don't stop," I urged pushing hard down on his head thrusting my pelvis up and down in rhythm with his mouth. Spasming jolts seized my body underneath him he held such skill.

"Oh Jayce," I yelled out in gratification from the best orgasm I had ever felt but we were far from done.

"Now go sit on the recliner and keep your arms to the sides. You're not allowed to move," I proclaimed positioning my self in a sitting stance on my bed.

"You're in charge," he smirked wiping me off of his face walking over to the recliner taking his seat.

I reached into my nightstand drawer and pulled out my favorite rabbit toy and then took it down my my throat to moisten it. Not that I really needed to I was already still soaking wet down below.

Jayce's eyes widened in excitement watching me closely.

I placed it down into my depths leaning back into my pillow slowly starting to slide it in and out. Intensely I increased my speed ramming the vibrator deep inside turning it on as the rabbit ears teased at my nub. With my free hand I starting taking turns rubbing circles over each nipple hardening them before his needy eyes.

I looked over to Jayce panting profoundly joyously taking pleasure in my own hands. I watched Jayce grab hold of his large stiff member ready to stroke it he was so desperate to feel the sensations I was inflicting on myself.

"No! you're not allowed to touch yourself. Put your hands back on the arms sitting there being a good boy watching the show," I yelled at him in defiance halting from my actions.

"But Mia," he whimpered.

"But nothing, you're going to do as you're told or I can make things a lot worse." I wanted to make him suffer for hurting me even though it was unintentional. He should have at least told me what he was up to but he didn't and now he was paying for it.

"Fine," he complied with a grunt of disapproval heeding my asserted threat.

I kept fucking myself with my play toy while I made him tortuously watch defenseless until I met with another gratifying climax. This time I screamed out louder than the first time when he ate away at me.

I placed the rabbit back into my drawer and got up walking over to Jayce. Immediately he reached out trying to pull me down on to him but I jolted back slapping his hands back down to the arms of the chair.

"How many times am I going to have to tell you? You're not allowed to move unless I tell you otherwise," My eyes burned into his with an evil seriousness spread across my face.

"You're fucking killing me," he cried with his body twitching he was in such desperate need to be touched.

"Good," I smirked with content.

I took his hard stiff member from the opening hole in his briefs grasping it tightly in my hand with his tip still exposed. I let my tongue only graze the top swirling it around as I took in small sucks. I don't think I had ever felt someone grow so stiff his erect dick was rock solid. Oh this was going to feel real good inside me.

Jayce tilted his head back moaning in misery and delight as he dug his nails into the arms of the recliner in a frustrated sexual frenzy.

"You're being a good boy, do want me fuck you now?" I teased with a devilish smirk.

"Yes, yes, please fuck me," he begged with a pleading lust.

I let out an evil chuckle before I pulled down his boxers tossing them aside. He was so dry I wrapped my mouth over top taking him down my throat several time to make sure he could easily be slid into my entrance while I stroked his shaft.

His breathing had become harsh hitching back and forth struggling for air only feeling the smallest of pleasures craving for more.

Finally I straddled myself on top of him guiding his member inside my wet dripping crease. Fuck! It felt so good to finally have my walls tightening around him. I knew I should have grabbed a condom but I needed so desperately to feel him raw for once.

A deep exhale left him as I started circling and grinding in a slow steady precision.

"You can touch me now," I leaned my mouth just below his ear whispering through my panting breathes.

"Thank you," finally relieved he cupped one ass cheek yanking me into him driving himself into me further. Then he took my right breast in his other hand holding it up into his mouth sucking hard on my nipple making my breast ache in bliss.

When he pulled away from my breast I moved in to his lips crashing into them with mine inhaling his habit-forming kisses. How I missed them always consistently yearning for more.

I started hammering up and down with force thrusting harder and harder as I dug my nails deep into his shoulders feeling the heated flames burn inside me turning into a wildfire. I rammed myself on top of him now with rapid speed I could feel my spot being hit while our mouths brutally ravaged one another's.

Fucking him felt so good I climaxed not once but two more times almost ready to reach gratification again until Jayce interrupted.

"Mia, I'm going to cum now, you need to get off of me,' he hesitantly warned.

I pulled myself off of him and dropped down to my knees looking up into his steel blue eyes. " I want you to finish on me," I seductively offered.

With that his white mess shot across my face falling onto to my chest trickling down my bosoms as I licked my lips to take in a taste.

I just looked up at him and smiled the naughtiest of grins, him looking down smiling back.

CHAPTER 9

S ecretly Jayce started sleeping in my bed every night since the would be poker game once we would hear Tyler go down to his room for the night. With the doors locked all he had to do was just get up and return to his room if we heard Tyler making his way up the steps in the morning.

He had been currently staying with us for over three weeks and I was starting to get the feeling his apartment was now livable again but he didn't want to go back yet which I didn't mind.

We had discussed how different things would be if he went back home. It would become really difficult to see each other considering everyone knew where he lived and would frequently pop by unannounced. We hadn't figured out much of anything if living arrangements changed unless we finally told Tyler which was something I didn't think I could ever be ready to do but the thought always crossed my mind. I knew no matter what that it was going to be a huge mess when Tyler found out, a mess I wasn't ready to deal with but one that was inevitable and complicating my relationship more and more the longer the secret remained.

Luckily this week Tyler made arrangements to go out of state with his father for a family outing three states away in North Carolina. No more lies and sneaking around for once, finally, me and Jayce were getting the opportunity to roam around the house freely without fear. Mmm and naked if we wanted, that was a refreshing revelation.

I woke up in bed with with my arm curled around Jayce's waist and my head resting on his hairless naked chest. His heated body pressed against mine in warmth making me let out a small grin of content as I pulled myself in tighter. I loved waking up in his arms every morning hating it when he'd have to eventually leave but for once this time he didn't have to since Tyler had already left yesterday afternoon.

"Mmm, hey you," Jayce softly spoke looking down at me with his eyelids starting to peer open.

"Hey," I looked up with an illuminating glow as he took his arm around me pulling me in closer to his body. I couldn't stop smiling so enamored I had finally found someone in my life who truly made me happy and sincerely cared for me.

"So what are we going to do today beautiful?" He asked just before he placed a gentle kiss on the top of my hair.

"Can we just stay in bed for awhile? It's nice not having you need to sneak off back in your room as as soon as we get up." I think I could just lay there all day comfortably wrapped in his tender arms probably never wanting to get up with his hold bringing me such solace.

Jayce turned over pulling himself over top of me and gently started suckling at my lips while he lifted my shirt up and then off exposing my naked flesh. "How about..." and then he paused pinning my arms up above the pillow with my shirt now down to the floor, "we..." another silent break came as his head had moved down and he began trailing kisses in between each breast, "watch some porn.. and then...(more kisses fell between his slowly spoken words).. reenact each scene?" and he then continued back to tenderly caressing my upper body with his moist lips.

"I juuust don't think I'm there yet," I chuckled nodding my head up and down raking my fingers through his hair not taking him seriously. Serious or not though I'm pretty sure if I did say yes he wouldn't object.

"Okay, we'll do that on Tuesday,"smirking he lifted himself back up meeting my lips once again with his.

"Haha," I dryly replied after our kiss broke considering it was Monday morning. Jayce sometimes had me questioning what was more difficult, raising a young man or sleeping with one.

"I'm good with just staying in bed for a while," he softly smiled resting his head down on my chest. His arms curled around me as I wrapped my arms back around him stroking the bare flesh on his backside with one hand, my fingers lightly massaging. I ruffled my fingers through his hair with my other hand closing my eyes indulging in the moment. Easily we fell back asleep spooned in each other without having to fear being discovered.

"Okay Mia, it's time to get up," I felt Jayce starting to shake my shoulder as I lay balled up facing the left edge of the bed not wanting to open my eyes.

"No, I don't want get out of bed," I wined childishly like a five year old toddler and then I took the blanket over my head trying to hide underneath. "Go away boogieman, I want Jayce back," I whimpered some more.

"Mia you can be such a goof. Come on please? I have something I want to show you," at first Jayce chuckled and then changed his tone to a more serious nature pleadingly.

"Fine," I huffed out in defeat taking the blanket back down over my face. When I looked over to Jayce he was already showered and dressed. When the hell did he do all that and how long had I been sleeping?

"Go get washed up and meet me downstairs," he said leaving me really curious. That woke me up.

"What, what is it?!" I asked enthusiastically springing up to a seated position now ready to leap out of bed I was so excited. I loved surprises but just like a kid I was also very impatient dying to know what he had hidden from me.

"Well if you'd get that sexy butt of yours up from bed you'll find out. Now get in that bathroom and I'll see you in about twenty five minutes," he affirmed placing a small peck on my cheek before getting up and striding off towards downstairs.

I brushed my teeth and showered in less than five minutes, dried my hair as fast as I could, and then threw on a blue and white cotton floral printed summer dress. Oh how I loved those summer dresses, they were comfortable, cute, and convenient.

Anxiously I ran down the steps as soon as I was all cleaned up finding Jayce seated at the dining room table when I made my way past the living area. The table was covered with a unique assortment of items each containing a post-it attached with a short note written on it. Everything was spread out as if in an order leading closer to Jayce.

He just sat there quietly observing me while I got to the first piece of the puzzle.

Item 1: a coloring book with crayons

Note: because you're young at heart never letting age define you

I smiled and let out a chuckle (I was so going to use this always embracing the kid in myself)

Item 2: a bucket of sugar cookies from the mall

Note: because you're so sweet and delicious

and now I was beginning to blush

Item 3: a handful of Hershey's Kisses

Note: Because your kisses are like chocolate melting in my mouth

my cheeks turning even redder by this point feeling a heated flush

Item 4: A fresh white rose

Note: because like this flower you are beautiful and so full of life (okay the flowers going to die but you get my point :))

that last one now leaving me laughing and almost crying I was so taken back

It took me a moment before I could find the words to say. The butterflies tingled all over my body I was so blown away and in awe by this welcomed surprise. I had never had anyone do something so romantic and well thought out for me before. All my insecurities stood non-existent at that moment feeling like I was a princess standing on a pedestal being worshiped by Prince Charming. It's then I finally knew I had completely fallen head over heels for him. Somehow Jayce had reached into unobtainable depths inside my soul I thought I had kept heavily guarded and stolen my heart.

I walked over to Jayce and straddled myself over his lap facing forwards with a slight tear now sliding down my cheek.

"Why are you crying, don't you like it?" he asked in worry.

"I love it, thank you," I replied as I wrapped my arms around his neck and moved in for a kiss. Our mouths met in unison with his arms locking around my waist slowly melting me in his grasps.

With our lips still unbroken Jayce cupped my behind with both hands and lifted us up from the chair never breaking away from our kiss taking us up the steps.

"There's somewhere I was planning to take you today but it can wait. I want to make love to you right now," his intense eyes seared through me filled with affection as he sat me down on the bed slowly undressing me.

Was that his way of telling me he loved me? I was speechless afraid to ask, afraid to hear the actual words said, and afraid to say them myself. My emotions were spiraling out of control inside of me, I was happy, scared, excited, but worst of all, I was in love the one thing I feared the most knowing it was eventually going to be my undoing.

I didn't move just letting him take control undressing before me after I had been stripped of my clothes pushing my fears aside. The moment was too perfect to let my paranoia ruin it.

He handled me delicately laying me out on the bed hovering above me. He began applying his wet lips against my neck gently suckling as he ran the outside of his fingers up and down my side just inches away from my breast down to my waist.

My heart raced as his mouth trailed down my body with butterfly kisses leaving the nape of my neck until his kisses reached my inner thighs. His fingers met my fold fondling it in circular motions as his head looked upwards, "Mia you're mine now, you belong to me."

"Jayce, I..I.." I stuttered through my panting breath still in fear of letting those three words escape me.

"Shhh," he hushed me, "You don't need to say anything right now," he whispered calmly.Then he took his long hardened shaft into my entrance gracefully with slow but meticulous strides. Each thrust was made in precision with little force filled with passion not lust for the first time.

When I met my climax it didn't just feel like I was being sexually gratified. It was like somehow I had just been completed bringing me to a new unfamiliar pleasure that outweighed any other I had encountered in my life. I don't think I ever really knew what it felt like to be made love to, that was at least until now.

CHAPTER 10

The Last word still hadn't been discussed but I knew what we had just done wasn't just sex. I avoided bringing it up as we got redressed to go out for another surprise Jayce had planned. I knew if I let the words come out of my mouth I wouldn't be able to take them back making it so much more real. It wasn't that I didn't relish in the idea that we could be happy together but the fear of the next step was what was overwhelming me.

"Oh Tyler by the way, me and Jayce are having sex but it's okay because we're in love," and then the WBAL news broadcast would flash through my head next. "Breaking news at 5:00, another violent murder hits Baltimore County, some say it was a crime of passion, some say it was domestic violence that played a part. Details still yet unknown."

"Mia!" I heard Jayce yell breaking me away from my obscure nightmare.

"Sorry, my mind has a way of getting away from me," I complied obviously shaken up as my words came out distant.

"What's wrong, is it something I did? You can talk to me you know," he took hold my of hand gently caressing my skin with his as we stood by the front door ready to leave.

"Is this because I told you I love you?" He pried even deeper opening up the discussion I wanted to avoid and at the same time clearly confessing his love without uncertainty.

"Come on, let's sit and talk," he didn't give me chance to respond leading us over to the sofa seating us down while he still stroked the top of my hand with his.

"I love you too," the sentiment finally released but the tears followed immediately after streaming down my cheeks.

"But you love Tyler and you're worried because you know we really have to tell him now," his words were filled with compassion and understanding.

"Yea, I'm so scared of how this is going to affect him. Being in love shouldn't be so complicated but somehow it is and it sucks." I was in admiration as his soothing affection warmed me throughout but I couldn't even revel in it I was too disturbed.

"Just remember, Tyler never played a part in us meeting. We did that on our own. There was no way either of us could have seen any of this coming that night. I just knew when I woke up that morning and you were gone I was at a loss. I've had my one night stands but for some reason I couldn't forget about you. You were so strong and commanding, you weren't afraid to do or say what you wanted. You were unlike any other woman I've known or would ever meet. The only thing I've ever seen you afraid of is hurting Tyler which only draws me into you even more." Then he held his hands out mid air with his head nodding, " and the sex, you could put porn stars to shame, not that I'm talking from experience of course. I'm only going by what I've seen on the internet."

"Damn you Jayce," I chuckled wiping away my tears,"you always have a way of cheering me up even when I don't know if I want to be."

"We have a couple of days left before he get's back home. We'll figure things out by then but now it's our time to enjoy ourselves without worry," he offered reassuringly as he brushed a strand of hair behind my ear kissing away my tears. I dissolved under his lips heeding his words. We only had a couple of more days left and I needed to make the most of them. His power over me always clouding my decisions having me following my heart which in our case wasn't necessarily always the right choice.

" Okay, but where are you taking me? What if somebody sees us?"

"Mia sometimes your paranoia makes me wonder if you don't have a bomb shelter hidden underneath this house. My friend's don't hang out at this place, we'll be fine." He laughed.

"Do you have a bomb shelter underneath?" he playfully added back in trying to act serious.

"Fine, and no, I couldn't afford the bomb shelter. It was too expensive," I joked batting my lashes. I was a paranoid freak but I trusted him knowing better that he would take us somewhere it was unlikely to be seen. I guess I just needed some reassurance.

"See, all better now. Now we can go," and then he gave me a minute to straighten myself back up and we headed out the door.

We left the house and got into his oversized SUV. I tried asking where he was taking me to on the way there but he wouldn't budge an inch. I just watched from the passenger side window of his Escalade staring out noticing that he were headed towards the city. Jayce drove through the Harbor tunnel entering downtown with all it's bright lights, tall buildings and crowded streets. He drove straight through making his way to the Inner Harbor until he pulled up to some exquisite restaurant sitting right on the water.

"I thought you might like a change from pizza in bed," he brightly smiled as he took my hand escorting me out of the vehicle while the valet took over in the driver's seat.

"This is definitely a step up from pizza in bed but can you afford this?" I knew he didn't work and his father paid all of his bills so he could focus on school like Mark and I did for Tyler but I had never bothered to ask much further into it and this place seemed pretty pricey.

"Let's just say I know the owner real well now come on, I'm hungry." he evasively replied.

I followed him in, I figured I'd just grill some answers out of him during dinner because he definitely had some explaining to do.

Everyone there immediately knew who he was greeting him as Mr. Montgomery peaking my curiosity. Who was he? Some secret agent?

I waited to start asking questions until the food was brought out to us. I was too caught up in the the calming atmosphere and enchanting scenery. We were sat out on the patio at a private table that overlooked the water underneath the twinkling stars. The full moon gleamed just above the harbor hailing over the small ships settled underneath. I don't think I had ever seen such a beautiful view of the harbor before, everything was so perfect and romantic. How did I get so lucky from what was meant to be just a one night stand?

"Okay Jayce, are you some kind of 007 I don't know about?"

"No," he chuckled, "My father owns this restaurant and a couple others. That's why I'm majoring in business so I can work with him once I graduate," he replied while he cut into his steak.

"Oh," I hung my head down in dismay putting down my silverware.

"What's wrong, why does that seem to upset you?" I had halted him from his meal with concern.

"I just realized I'm suppose to be in love with you and there's so many things I don't even know about you." I felt like an idiot, these several weeks I had gotten to know Jayce but I hadn't really gotten to know Jayce. I knew that when I was sad he could always put a smile on my face, when I needed comfort he was there to hold me in his arms and sooth my soul with his embrace, I knew that my pulse raced ten times faster whenever I felt his touch, but I barely knew anything about the life he had outside of me.

"You know I love you and all the little stuff that comes after can be filled in," and that's what we did during the rest of our meal, fill in the blanks.

He told me more about his family and left out his mother which I already knew enough about. I'm glad he chose not to talk about her because I didn't like the way he got upset when he was brought back down that dark path. Any woman that abandoned their children didn't deserve the right to be called a mother. I didn't know her but I knew I didn't have to to know I hated her.

It turned out Jayce's father owned several fancy restaurants in Maryland that Jayce was going to help run when he finished college. His sister Andrea and him were very close with her being 3 years younger but she was currently living out of state going to school in Michigan studying law. She had come home briefly at the beginning of the summer but returned to Michigan to focus on some extra studying leaving the night before we met.

I didn't really have much to tell him, I just sat back mainly and listened. He already knew everything there was to know about me from the time he spent at the house. There wasn't much more to learn about me that he hadn't already from living at my home day in and out.

After we were done eating I felt so much closer to him now that I knew more about his family and his life.

"Thank you for dinner, it was beautiful," I said with a beaming ora surrounding me gazing into his capturing blue eyes while we made our way out the front doors. I couldn't help but feel those tingling sensations constantly inflamed inside when I was around him. The sweet things he did, the way his touch sent electricity coursing through my veins every time, I had never felt more enamored or alive.

"Well you know the night's not over yet. I know how much you love to dance, there's an exclusive club around the corner that I'm taking you to next." I was always listening to dance music around the house unable to stay still. I guess it wasn't to hard for him to catch onto how I loved to move to music.

I just smiled and rested my head on his shoulder as he locked his arm with mine and lead us down the street.

When we entered the club the multicolored lights flickered back and forth across the ceiling as the blaring speakers pulsated in our ears. The room was filled with individuals scattered all over either trying to make way through the crowds or grinding their bodies on the dance floor.

"You stay here and I'll grab us some drinks real quick," he yelled out to me over the loud trance beats that captivated the room.

"Okay," I replied still unable to stop glowing in his presence as he broke away heading to the bar off in the corner.

Shortly after Jayce walked off I felt someone grab onto my waist pulling me out on the dance floor gyrating against me.

"Come on baby, have some fun with me," a young stranger called out to me as he gripped his hands on my sides grinding himself into my body. I could tell straight off the bat that he was some sort of playboy that frequented the clubs attracting naive young women to go home with him for the night. His overconfidence, good looks, and designer clothing giving it away in an instance.

"I'm sorry, I'm here with somebody," I tried pulling away but he wouldn't break his hold.

"You're not going to try to lie to me and tell me you're here with your boyfriend are you? I'm sure your girlfriends won't mind us getting to know each other, they can wait an extra minute." He looked down at me locking his arm around me tightly with a grin of confidence. What a conceited ass.

I pulled away again this time freeing myself from his grip, "Actually I am here with....." and then I drew a blank. Jayce and I had never established any labels. Was he my boyfriend?

"She's here with me. Her boyfriend," Jayce asserted coming up from behind handing me my beer and then grabbed me with force curling his arm around my waist bringing us less than an inch apart. Without hesitation he fiercely started kissing me sparking that yearning twitch in between my legs he was so good at igniting. I guess he was my boyfriend which the new found knowledge only enlightened me more.

Our tongues twirled around each others as he would break away sporadically tasting my lips in his ever other second coming back in to let our tongues meet again with burning desire. I was lost in his mouth completely forgetting about the playboy who apparently got the point and had disappeared. I could feel his large member begin to stiffen as his body pressed hard against me tweaking my arousal.

Finally our kiss broke and we were moving into each other under the palpitating sounds. With my arms now wrapped around his neck I couldn't help but whisper in his ear, "I love you."

"I love you too..... Maybe we should get out of here and head home," I could tell the same insatiable lust I was feeling he was feeling too.

"Let's go."

Chapter 11

When we got home we landed straight up in my bedroom, we preferred mine since I had the queen sized bed.

"Jayce I want you handle me roughly tonight, I want you to be in charge this time," it was my turn to be submissive and frolic under his dominance. No more making love for now, I wanted to feel his experience rush inside, my appetite for him was rapacious needing to be conquered and put down.

"Is that so?" he radiated with his diabolical grin peering from his face. Then he took both of his hands to my chest ripping my dress down at the seams until the tear fell below my breasts causing my dress to fall to my feet. I didn't mind that my dress had just been ruined, it could easily be replaced unlike the moment.

Flashing bolts of lightening scoured throughout every inch of me as I gasped in a deep breath in shock and excitement while my body shuddered.

Then just when I thought I couldn't be surprised again so quickly he grabbed onto my hair tugging my head back hard and started ravaging my neck with juicy filled lips. I could feel his wet tongue sliding around not only soaking my neck but soaking that crease below that loved being violated by him.

"Fuck Jayce, whatever's taken over you I'm loving it," I moaned reaching down to the button of his pants anxiously undoing them and taking down the zipper. I grabbed onto his hard manhood and started stroking with fervency.

"You've taken over me, you're mine remember," not a question but a statement he panted.

My heart was racing so rapidly it felt like it was trying to stampede out of my chest. Oh god, it only ever seemed to get better with each sexual experience that I encountered with him.

"Are you wet for me baby?" he asked as he took his mouth down to my breast taking in a sharp bite over top of the cotton of my bra.

"Mmmm yes, so wet I think I could flood a whole country," his piercing teeth causing me a joyous pain that started crashing waves to course throughout my body.

Jayce chuckled at my sentiment and then pulled back making me let go of my grip. "I have an idea. Take off your undergarments and I'll be right back," I didn't ask , he walked off to his bedroom knowing I was going to enjoy whatever it was he had planned.

When he entered back his broad naked body was exposed with two neck ties perched in his hand. Oooh, I think I was really going to like this.

I said nothing, he approached back demanding me to lay down. I complied nervously trembling anxious as to what was to come next.

He got on the bed lifting my head and blindfolded me with the first tie. With my eyes now masked, my head back rested on the pillow, he took the other tie tightly knotting it around my wrists and positioned my arms above my head.

At this point my body was quivering. My sex was frustrated stuck in a sexual frenzy.

"Are you ready for me?" he taunted.

"Yes, yes, yes," I desperately begged. No foreplay was needed I was dying inside needing him to bring me back to life.

"Then what am I waiting to hear?"

I knew exactly what he wanted, he wanted to hear me beg saying his name proving his power over me right then and there.

"Yes, Jayce, please....I want you now, I need to feel you now," I pleaded feeling myself starting to sweat I was so aroused.

"I'm glad you haven't forgot who's in charge," he whispered into my ear, his heated breath radiated onto my skin.

I could feel him take hold of his solid member navigating it to my empty space that needed to be filled.

"Fuck yes," I bellowed out a loud moan while he stuffed himself inside of me. His lips took in mine as he abrasively hammered away at my sacred ground. My body convulsed underneath, his thrashing pounds making way deeper and deeper pushing into my depths.

"Shit Mia, you're so fucking wet right now. It feels so good with you locked around my dick," he moaned with his breath gasping just as fast as mine.

My flesh burned hotter than fire with flames only he could extinguish with him ramming faster and faster, my walls tightening in. I wanted to touch him but it also felt good being so defenseless with my arms still restrained above my head.

"Fuck!" I screamed out finally hitting my crest of utter satisfaction.

Minutes later Jayce followed with a loud groan pulling himself out making sure he left his mark all over my chest then dropped down besides me still trying to catch his breath.

"Wow," he said removing the ties staring at me in exhaustion with his brows furrowed.

"Wow," I grinned looking back at him letting out a rooted exhale.

CHAPTER 12

After our "Wows" we just started laughing in amusement while we lay there naked fully exposed and then we heard the knock at the door disturbing our little moment.

I jumped startled by the sound at first thinking it could be Tyler but realized it couldn't be considering he was hundreds of miles away and why the hell would he knock at his own door when he had a key? But who was knocking on door at almost midnight? Beth, it had to be. I didn't know anyone else who always carried such bad timing.

"Do you want me to get it since you're a little messy right now?' Jayce smirked over to me.

"No, I'll just have to throw my robe in the wash with the rest of my dirty laundry tomorrow," I said giving him a smug look.

"It's Beth anyways, you know how she is." I replied letting out a deep breath.

"Yea I do, that means no seconds," he scowled hanging his head down depressingly now sitting perched up with his back rested against the headboard.

I got up grabbing my girly cotton robe off the bathroom door throwing it on and walked back over to Jayce leaning in giving him a kiss. "I promise I'll get rid of her fast, I swear and there'll be seconds," I guaranteed wincing.

Jayce reached out grabbing my arm pulling me back down on his hard mass of a shell physique, "Just ignore her and she'll go away, stay up here with me and we can take a shower together. You know if you answer that door she's not going to leave. Please, please, please?" He started batting his lashes and giving me the sad puppy dog eyes. He had gotten to know Beth as well as he knew me.

I lay hovered over top of him combing his silky brown hair through my fingers taking in his manly scent gently kissing all over his face. I was just about to give in as the idea of a shower together sounded irresistibly inviting but then I heard the yell bellow out with more rapid pounding following behind, "Mia, I know your ass is in there!" Beth's voice blared throughout the house breaking pass the door.

"She's relentless, I better answer," and then I lifted myself back up and started walking towards the hallway.

"Hey, you better get rid of her," Jayce called out tossing a pillow at me nailing me in my side.

"Owe, you're going to pay for that," I sneered as I turned slightly to face him picking the pillow up off the floor and threw it back at him.

He just swatted it down back onto the bed laughing, "Then make me pay beautiful," he seductively retorted lifting one eyebrow with the corner of his mouth breaking into a smile.

I just chuckled veering my head back around and kept going. If I stayed upstairs any longer Beth would probably break the door down.

As soon as I opened the front door Beth's face widened with a wicked smirk, "You just got laid you naughty girl," she cooed.

"Just because I'm in a robe doesn't mean I just had sex. Your minds just always in the gutter." I tried defending myself with a meaningless lie. I knew I couldn't hide the illumination that followed such a joyous experience.

"Hooker please, it's not the robe that gave it away. You're glowing brighter than a fucking Christmas tree," and then she turned her head facing the steps with her hand pressed by her mouth to echo her voice, "Hi Jayce," she called out.

"I hate you Beth," Jayce dryly yelled back down the steps hearing the disappointment in his voice making it clear Beth had impeccably bad timing.

Beth just started laughing as I grinned.

"Yup he's definitely a keeper," she kept laughing as she let herself in the front door and then walked over to the sofa plopping herself down comfortably without a care in the world.

"Can I help you with something?" I looked to her sarcastically shutting the front door.

"You haven't been taking any of my texts or calls for days. I was starting think Tyler had finally caught you guys and something bad had happened," her enlightened mood now switching to a more serious nature.

"Sorry," I walked over taking a seat on the black recliner adjacent to her. "I've just been really busy with stuff. Tyler went away with his dad for a little bit so I'm safe for the time being." I reassured her.

I had been so wrapped up with Tyler and Jayce I hadn't thought of cluing her in, if I had maybe I'd be in the shower right now instead of entertaining her.

"I see that now. No wonder you weren't taking my calls," she snickered bobbing her head up and down raising a brow.

At that Jayce made his way down the steps in just his boxers with his outlined upper torso garnishing attention making him as drool worthy as ever.

"I knew you weren't going to be able to get rid of her," dramatically he cut in coming up behind me at the recliner and hung his arms down over my shoulders leaning in placing a gentle kiss on the side of my face. I took hold of one his arms clutching onto it and rubbed my fingers down his thick formed build going back and forth with my other hand. It was something so simple but I loved touching him as much I loved being touched by him, even if it was just his arms hanging over my shoulders that connected us.

"Awe, you to two are so cute," Beth taunted. She knew what was going on but with all the sneaking around that was the first time she had actually witnessed us showing our affection for one another.

"Well Beth it was so nice of you to stop by but Mia's tired and needs her rest. She'll give you a call tomorrow," he tried coercing her to leave.

"I am tired Beth. I'm sorry I had you so worried but we should head off to bed right now." I let out a fake yawn bringing my hand to my mouth but I wasn't really tired. What I was was really sticky underneath my pink cotton robe wanting to get washed up and not without assistant.

"Okay, okay, I'm leaving, I get the point. I'm just glad everything is alright. I'll let you two lovebirds go back at it now," she giggled then finally got up making her way to the front.

"I'll call you tomorrow, I promise," I told her as she started exiting the house.

"You better bitch. See you guys later."

"See ya."

"Bye Beth," Jayce added in right before Beth left shutting the door behind her. Yes! Alone again at last.

Not that I didn't appreciate Beth being so concerned that she felt the need to show up even if it was the middle of the night, I just wanted to take full advantage of my alone time with Jayce.

Jayce crouched down so his mouth met my ear, "I told you so, you should have never answered the door," he teased.

"I didn't want to seem rude, she was just worried about me," I looked over to face him about to keep up the argument but then I started getting lost in his baby blues. Damn, he held some kind of power over me that made me easily forget the world around us. Thoughts of Beth quickly began to diminish as thoughts of Jayce and me being in the shower danced around in my head.

"Well...." before he could finish his sentence I cut him off.

"Shut up and stop arguing with me when we could be in the tub right now," I grimaced devilishly raising my brows and puckering my lips.

That seemed to make him happy because with that he moved around the recliner taking my hand and pulling me up to my feet, "Well what are you waiting for?" and then he led us up the steps grinning cheek to cheek as I complied.

Immediately I dropped my robe and Jayce slipped out of his boxers when we made our way into the bathroom. Jayce began running the water adjusting it to the perfect temperature as I grabbed two towels from the linen closet for the two of us placing them on the rack.

He stepped in first reaching out offering me his hand so I could follow. I gladly accepted his invitation positioning myself in front of his naked masculine form with my back facing him feeling his hand fall to my chest lathering me with a soap filled sponge.

My back arched with a curl as my head faltered back onto the crook of his neck. My eyes closing shut savoring each movement his hand made lathering me up over top of my cleavage while it concluded it's way down onto my stomach before reaching my fold. If there was truly a heaven on earth then I was there already underneath his grips.

"Oh Jayce," I called out in a whisper hitching my breath.

"I love hearing you say my name," he rejoiced in a devious tone soaping what lay between my inner thighs with vehemence.

The friction between my crease and the lathered sponge sent spasming currents throughout my body causing me to squeal in jubilance and glee.

Vigorously the tension increased until I moaned out in a fulfilled delight meeting yet another one of the many apexes he inflicted on me.

"Did you like that baby?" he contented.

I rolled my head around from his neck to face him taking in his lips as my reply. I lapped my tongue from top to bottom until bringing it into his mouth meeting with his. I had fallen into a trap with no release being held prisoner under his command. Never could I have ever fathomed pleasures he brought to me truly existed if I hadn't experienced them for myself.

The heated pellets of water trickled down our bodies as our lips stayed locked and his hands traced all over my front side with the sponge now fallen to the ground. I couldn't help but let out gasping moans as his fingers massaged my breasts causing my back to arch out more.

"Are you going to do sex to my body?," I playfully slipped out between our mouths.

His lips curled into a smile behind mine, "Only if you really want me to," he baited as he moved in closer letting me feel his hard member brush up against my buttocks.

"I think you already know the answer to that," I replied never moving away from his lips.

With that he pivoted our bodies around so we were both facing the back of the tub and maneuvered my hands up against the wall. His hands glided down from mine moving underneath my arms brushing past my breasts until they reached just below my waist provoking the convulsing eruptions inside me. With a gentle tug he positioned me in a hunched stance ready to take him in.

My body twinged eagerly before him as he began to fondle my fold in his fingers with one hand while his other prepared his thick manhood to make way inside of me.

His mouth moved in towards my neck devouring the lobe of my ear as he suckled on it and then softly spoke, "then let me hear you say it," he enticed.

"Fuck me Jayce," I let out almost cold but stern.

He complied without indecisiveness sliding his wet member inside my empty yearning spot. The first thrust came with resilience followed by forceful increasing blows as I could feel his pelvis smacking into me from behind.

I tightened in around him moaning and panting in elation biting down on my bottom lip trying to contain my sanity as his veiny muscle drove me wild.

"Oh God Mia, how is it you always feel so fucking unbelievable!" he called out grunting struggling to speak as his voice turned rasp.

"Just don't stop, please don't stop," I begged never wanting the heated sensations that traveled throughout my body to ever come to an end.

"You make it hard to keep going," he let out fighting to stay in control of his body as he hammered into me more.

I knew he wouldn't be able to contain himself for much longer so I reached down and started rubbing on my clit back and forth firmly.

"Just a little bit longer," I pleaded bringing myself in closer towards completion.

He grabbed onto my hair balling it in his hand tugging hard increasing the pounding thrusts desecrating what sat between my legs, "I don't know if I can," you could hear the disparity.

That was exactly what I needed to hit my heightened peak as I moaned out a loud, "Yes," in relief.

"Ahhhh, Fuck!" he cried out with a deep exhale meeting his solitude in unison with mine pulling out just in time.

Turns out I needed to get washed again but it was worth it.

CHAPTER 13

J ayce had made me dinner, spaghetti, something so sweet and simple but because it was Jayce cooking we ended up ordering Chinese. Bonus points for the effort, I was still swept away by the gesture even though the noodles were crispy when I bit in and it ended up in the garbage disposal. During dinner We had decided when Tyler got home that Jayce would return to his apartment so I could speak to Tyler alone and make my confession. We both agreed it would be best if this was something I did by myself knowing Tyler wasn't going to take it well and with Jayce in the room it would only aggravate Tyler more. Then we just took in a movie and went to bed early exhausted from all our extra curricular activities that kept us preoccupied most of the time with only two days left of freedom. The other night was the only time we had gone out in public with me still being hesitant worried about being discovered so we stayed home the rest of the week enjoying each other behind closed doors.

"What the fuck! I knew it!" The words pierced through my heart repetitively jabbing like a knife as soon as I heard his voice with the door flinging open forcefully followed by a loud thud smacking against the wall.

Jayce flung up from the bed in an instance standing practically naked in only his boxers walking towards him only making the situation worse.

"Tyler, you don't understand! It's not what you think," Jayce tried defending what looked like only betrayal to Tyler.

Fire scorched in Tyler's stare fueled by anger as he stood there fuming in rage while he looked up at Jayce with nothing but hatred behind his eyes. Jayce moved in closer trying to place a hand on Tyler's shoulder to try to calm him, try to explain, but Tyler was too outraged jerking a way forcing Jayce's hand to swing back in the air.

Then it came without warning, Wham! Tyler's balled up fist filled with fury quickly finding way to Jayces cheek. You could hear the smack of Tyler's blow meeting the flesh of Jayce's face as Jayce's head lobbed off to the side almost causing him to falter to the floor.

"Tyler please stop, give me a chance to explain!" I begged as I quickly got up from the bed taking a place in between the two men I loved standing only in a white tee and underwear intervening. Fear and pain conquered my entirety as I trembled in anguish. What I had dreaded was finally becoming a reality and in the worse way possible. Tyler had not only found out about me and Jayce now but he had to witness it so unprepared.

I extended my arm trying to take hold of my baby but he flinched not letting me make contact. "Don't! I can't even look at you right now." I had never seen such disappointment and distance laced across his face before.

"But baby there's so much you don't know or understand. Please let me talk to you," I begged reaching out to him trying to move in closer as the tears started to stream down my cheeks.

"I can't be around you right now. I'm leaving and staying with dad," the anger had gradually left his voice being replaced with disgust. His head nodded in disappointment as he shook it in dismay.

"Please don't go. Not like this," I desperately called out but Tyler just turned his back and walked away as I listened to him making his exit with the front door slamming behind him. My knees fell to the floor with my hands covering my sobbing wet face. An emptiness filled inside my chest as I could feel my heart shattering. The hollowness pitting inside of me was so excruciating I felt like I could throw up. Never had I felt so empty like I did at that moment in time, oh God, what have I done?

Jayce came up from behind wrapping his arms around my shaken empty shell of a person. We didn't move from the ground as I turned my head weeping into his chest uncontrollably catching a glimpse of his reddening swollen cheek.

"We'll fix this, I'll fix this," he tried consoling me but for the first time in my life I feared the damage I had done to my son could possibly be irreversible. I'd never had him look at me so coldly and so drawn away ever. If Tyler never forgave me I don't think I would be able to survive, I'd rather be dead than live a life feeling this kind of pain everyday.

"I don't know if this can be fixed. It was like I was a stranger to Tyler he was so distant and drawn back. I can't lose him, he's my world," I broke down with my eyes so swollen I could barely open them.

"Mia, he'll come around. He just needs time to take all of this in," Jayce's words brought me no comfort. If anybody knew my son it was me and that young man who had just walked out was unrecognizable consumed with grief and deceit. I didn't know if I'd ever be able to get back the bond we shared.

Jayce lifted me up in his arms taking me to the bed I was so weak and drained from all the weeping.

"Jayce your face, you need ice," I tried getting up so I could take care of him but I couldn't stop bawling.

"I'll get the ice. You just lay down and try to get some sleep. We'll deal with this in the morning," Jayce convinced me to get back down I was to distraught to try to comfort him when I couldn't even contain myself. I cried all night until eventually falling asleep with Jayce tenderly by my side attempting to console me from my withered state.

"How are you?" Jayce asked hovering above me brushing the loose strands of my hair away from my face so he could see the broken woman that lie besides him as I started to awake hours later with morning entering through the window.

I rolled over to face him, "Jayce you know I love you right?" This was it, the words I hoped I'd never have to speak were about to come out of my mouth.

"Yes, and you know I love you but I can hear a but coming next," he could sense my question was serving a purpose leading into something else.

"You have to leave today. You need to go back home now and not come back here." The emptiness in my chest grew more vacant with what had to be said.

"I know. It's going to be a while before I can come back over," he was misunderstanding my statement making this ten times harder then it already was.

"No Jayce, I love you but this is over," It pained me so much to say that, knowing this time it was really true. All those times before when I tried to push him away but kept giving in him leading me to this point where it was finally for real. I didn't want to end things but had I no choice, my son had made the decision for me.

"What are you talking about?" You could see the hurt and confusion sting through his eyes as he moved in closer wrapping one of his arms around me. He took his other arm bring his hand to my face cupping my cheek in his calloused fingers, "Mia, I don't know what your trying to say."

"It doesn't matter what we want anymore, what matters is getting my son back and I can't do that if we're together. This never should have continued and I blame myself. I should have never agreed to letting you stay here and none of this would have ever happened. Please don't make this harder than it already is," it killed me knowing we were done, that I would never taste his kiss, feel his warm embrace, run my fingers through his silky dark hair again. My heart was breaking already in a million pieces but now it felt like it was shattering into a million more.

"Us meeting that night at the bar and then finding you again the next day, that was fate and you can't deny it. There was something beyond our control bringing us together. You and me were meant to happen and I can't just let you go. I know things are going to be difficult for a while with Tyler but it doesn't mean you have to throw away what we have. We'll just have to keep a distance for some time until we can all work things out," his determination was making this so much harder as he grabbed onto my hand holding it to his chest real tight.

The tears started to trickle down my face again as I moved in placing a soft kiss on his lips," I'm going to take a long shower now and when I get out I need you to be gone," I pulled back my hand and got up walking towards the bathroom. I locked the door behind me and started the water but didn't get in. I just leaned my back up against the door and dropped down to the ground balling up crying with my knees drawn into my chest.

"Mia don't do this, open up the door," he yelled but I ignored his pleas as he banged hard on the door just whimpering into my knees with my arms curled around my legs.

"Damn it, open up the fucking door!," Jayce screamed with his fists almost breaking through the wood.

"Jayce please, just leave. I can't do this right now," I whimpered under my crying.

Jayce was persist, pounding and begging me to just let him in for at least 30 minutes but that was what started all of this in the first place, letting him in. I had let him into my home, my bedroom, my life, and my heart and it all came back to bite me in the ass. I just needed him to go or I was going to completely fall to pieces so I stayed in there for over an hour until I was sure he was gone. If this was fate then it was pretty twisted and fucked up. I felt nauseous and sick to my stomach unable to handle the piercing agony that stabbed into my soul so I grabbed two sleeping pills out of my nightstand taking them and got back into my bed.

My reality was a nightmare, my only hope of solace was in my slumber. I never wanted to wake up once I went to sleep because

I knew this wasn't going to get any better. Even if I did win back Tyler I had now lost Jayce forever.

CHAPTER 14

I lie there staring up at the ceiling with a closed smile, "Mommy why are you parking in the candy cane?" Tyler asked me as I parked the car in the mall lot pulling up in a marked space.

"No baby, you mean handicap," I chuckled at his innocence.

"Mommy why are you parking in the candy cap spot?" He asked again still not understanding at the young age of five.

"No silly, it's handicap and we're in the special spot just for mommies not the handicap," I laughed again correcting him one more time.

I could barely remember the things I did on a regular basis but my memories of 15 years ago played in my mind like a broken record when it came to Tyler.

My little boy always finding a way to brighten my day. I missed him so much as my lids began to water remembering back when I could do no wrong in his eyes.

Even though he was now in his twenties he would always end a phone conversation with I love and say the three words whenever he had to say goodbye, even if he was leaving for only an hour. The day he walked in on me and Jayce there was nothing, like he was trying to rip my heart out of my chest with his absence of words in retaliation. He always knew what things to do to strike a chord if he truly wanted revenge for something I did that made him upset.

"I love you," I spoke out loud before I closed my eyes trying to sleep once more not being able to bear the agony I was consumed with.

It had been a week and a half and Tyler refused to see me or take my calls. I had briefly spoken to his father coming to find out Tyler intentionally came home early from the family outing to confirm his hunches. I guess it hadn't been to difficult for Tyler to catch on to how Jayce and I looked at each other whenever we were in the same room together or how too close we always seemed.

Most days, actually everyday, I hid in my room balled up in my bed crying myself back to sleep. Jayce on the other hand was blowing me up like I was doing to Tyler. My phone would go off every hour ringing and chiming as I ignored each call and avoided opening up the messages because I knew if I read them I would eventually end up caving.

I wanted to talk to him, to see him, have him hold me in his arms and ease away the suffering but it wasn't allowed. For some reason the universe hated me causing me a grief no person should ever endure.

I couldn't sleep this time tossing and turning. I had already gotten too much rest as my body denied me more slumber. I was just about to grab some more sleeping pills and then I heard someone making there way up the steps.

"Mom?," the door opened with Tyler appearing behind it.

"Hey baby," I spoke softly so happy to finally see and hear my son call out to me. I wanted to walk over to him and caress him in my hold but I was afraid. The fear of his rejection once again would only be more devastating than before.

Tyler walked over to my bed taking a seat besides my frail weakened body, "Beth told me you weren't doing to well so I thought it was time I stopped by. You don't look to good, have you been eating?" Concern and love gazed from his eyes, my sweet boy still loved me, thank god.

"Yea," I lied not wanting him to worry. There were enough issues between us, I didn't need him concerned over my health when there were more important things that needed to be discussed.

The truth was I had barely eaten since I last saw him or Jayce, that emptiness in my chest overwhelmed my will to do anything.

"Tyler, I know what you saw looked bad but I met Jayce before you brought him over that day. I'm so sorry that we hid things from you until they spiraled out of control but I ended it. You're my life, please forgive me," I burst out before Tyler denied me the opportunity to give some kind of explanation.

" I don't want to hear about Jayce except for that it's over. You are really done right, you swear?" He still held that distance in his stare but not as far away as it once was.

"Yes, I promise," I couldn't go into detail how I was actually in love with Jayce, I knew Tyler wouldn't want to hear it. It would be to much. I feared he'd leave and never come back this time if I tried to win his approval over something I could never see him accepting; at least not after the way he had to find out.

"Good. Now get some rest and when you wake up you need to eat. You look like you've lost some weight. I love you." Tyler leaned over giving me a kiss on the cheek but quickly pulled away not ready to come to close.

"I love you too," the words finally spoken again giving me the smallest of relief and then I snuck off to get more sleeping pills to hide away. A milestone had just taken place but I was nowhere near better. I'm just glad Tyler hadn't realized all I did was rest to the point where I was forcing it on myself. I still felt that disparity that swelled throughout my entire core knowing I had only won back a piece of my son and still lost the man I loved.

Several weeks went by and things between Tyler and me gradually began to mend but I still maintained a gaping hole in my heart leaving me in the same state. I didn't eat, I didn't go out, I didn't leave my room still aching over Jayce.

Tyler mistook it as me coping with our situation which I let him believe as I did slowly begin to heal in more weeks to come but I was never truly the same person I use to be when Jayce was in my life.

Just as I found myself ready to finally leave my room and make an attempt to get back to the living Beth showed up which she had been doing more frequently trying to watch over me. The visit came as no surprise but what she brought and had to say did.

We both took a seat in the living room on the sofa with Beth holding something concealed in her bag.

"Mia, this is from Jayce. Since you won't take his calls and he can't stop by because of Tyler he came to me," Beth reached in her purse pulling out a coloring book and then handed it to me.

The tears began to swell at just the sight but then an outpour of drops followed when I opened up the cover to see what had secretly been buried inside the first page.

A yellow post-it reading: I love you, I miss you, please just talk to me Jayce

Beth just took me in her arms as I sobbed into her shoulder, "Mia this is destroying you. You're pale as a ghost and you've lost at least 10 to 15 lbs. You don't look well and Tyler's to blind and stubborn to see how much your not the person you use to be without Jayce," she stroked my hair trying to console and lecture me at the same time.

"You need to at least talk to him, he's not looking to good himself now a days. This is breaking his heart too. If I hadn't witnessed it for myself I would have never believed when I first met him that he was the one but you two were meant to be. I've never seen any man make you glow the way he does and give you so much life," Beth pleaded in Jayce's defense.

It warmed my heart knowing that he still carried the same affection I carried for him but it also hurt knowing I was also inflicting the same pain I encountered.

"I can't Beth, I just can't," was all I knew to say trying to hold back all the emotions that twisted and turned inside telling me to just give in and see him or at least call.

"You're drawing breath but it's like you're dead inside and out! Wake up and live your life for once. If Tyler loved you so much then why the fuck is he okay with killing you! You're letting your son dictate your entire life," Beth snapped freeing me from her arms and then stared into my eyes with a burning rage.

"Because Tyler is oblivious, he only sees what he wants to see so if loving my son is going to be the death of me then let it be!," I snapped back defending my child. I knew it wasn't lack of love, it was his ignorance and pride blinding him and his unwillingness to accept something he so strongly disapproved of nor understood.

"I'm sorry, I know Tyler loves you but so does Jayce," she calmed down in response. "I love you too Mia and it kills me seeing you like this."

"I know you do Beth, I'll be fine. I just need a little bit more time to heal that's all," I told her with a slight grin trying to be reaffirming.

Beth began to get up from the sofa striding towards the door ."Alright, I'll give you a little bit more time but if I don't see you getting better than things are going to change. I have to go now, I've got errands I need to take care of. I just wanted to stop by to check in on you and give you that book. Is there anything you want me to tell Jayce?," she asked before she made her way completely out of the front.

"No, I think you're right, I should call him if only just to say hello," I couldn't contain myself any longer. I just needed to hear his voice, know that he was fine.

"I'm glad to hear that, he'll be happy to finally hear from you," she smiled right before she left.

I picked up my cell phone from the coffee table in front of me and pulled up his name in my contacts. I hesitated for several minutes contemplating if it was such a good idea until I just swiped across the green call button not letting my racing thoughts get in the way.

I didn't even hear it ring once when I heard Jayce speak, "Mia?" Shock and joy jumbled up in one when he spoke my name.

"Hi," I said in a soft whisper. Listening to his husky voice just say my name brought me some consolation.

"I've missed you beautiful," he spoke tenderly but like a man who had been damaged. Damn it, I did this to him and I didn't know how to fix it.

"I've missed you too," and there it was, the tears flowing again down my face.

"Let me meet you somewhere or you can come over here. I need to see you, I can't take this anymore baby," he devotedly begged.

"Jayce you know I can't do that. I j...just, I j...ust wanted to hear your voice and know that you're doing alright. I should go now,"I stuttered as it wounded me to say these things but I needed to hang up before I did find myself driving over to his apartment.

"No Mia, please wait," he petitioned.

"I love you, goodbye," and then I ended the call drowning in my own tears as soon as I heard the phone cut off with only the sounds of my whimpers left to fill my ears.

Chapter 15

"Come on Mia, you're going out tonight!" Beth stormed into my room flinging the door open with impact almost putting a hole in the wall. The abrupt disturbance startling me in my bed causing my body to jump to a seated position but quickly calmed when I realized it was just her and not Lucifer to finally come claim my lifeless soul.

"Fuck off," I replied dryly giving her the middle finger and then threw the covers back over my head laying back down. I hadn't left the house in weeks and had no urge to, today was no different then any other.

"What the fuck!" I yelled out when I felt the quilted blanket pulled out from over me leaving me helpless under Beth's death stare. Her burning eyes stung into my half naked body wearing only a white t-shirt and pink laced underwear as I slightly shivered from the gust of air. This was one of those moments when I hated having a best friend who could be just as resilient and overbearing as me.

"Bitch I told you I'd give you some time and now your times up. You're getting out of this house and especially this bed even if I have drag you by the hair like a fucking caveman," she affirmed with her elbows cornered and her hands pressed firmly on the sides of her waists.

"Fred Flinstone could you please just give me back my blanket? I know you like the view but all I wanna do is sleep." It had been three days now since I had called Jayce and I was miserable beyond imagination. His pleading voice still echoing in my thoughts, a haunting reminder of how I was causing him so much pain only adding onto my misery. I'd been taking so many sleeping pills by this point that my tolerance had built up and I had to take an extra one just for them to work. Luckily for me there was online shipping so I never had to leave the house to refill my supply.

Jayce still made attempts to call and text but now I just shut off my phone completely to help avoid temptation. It wasn't like there was anyone I wanted or needed to talk to anyways besides him of course. I began to realize it wasn't Tyler that was stopping him from trying to come by, it was his loyalty and love for me that held him back. Jayce had to know another confrontation with him and Tyler would only devastate me more than I already was. I was thankful but it only made me miss Jayce more. Everyday was another struggle denying the best thing that had ever happened to me besides being a mother.

"You look like one of those starving kids on the television. Soon the neighbors are going to start leaving you canned goods outside the front door you look like shit. You're going to get your ass up, get dressed, and go out to eat with me and that's that! I'll give you 30 minutes to get ready then you can meet me and Tyler, we'll be downstairs waiting for you in the living room. He's coming too to make sure you eat even if he has to force feed you," she huffed whipping her blonde hair in the air as she turned around with attitude walking out ignoring my next argument.

I didn't really have much fight left in me anyways to keep trying to disagree with her so I guess it didn't matter that she let me be without listening to what I had to say. I got up from bed and took a quick five minute shower, dried up, then put on a pair of bootleg jeans and a floral embroidered tank top finishing it off with my black and turquoise DC tennis shoes.

I got downstairs and Beth and Tyler were silently awaiting for me both perched down on the sofa. It was as if they had heard me making my way down the steps quieting up like I had interrupted some discussion I wasn't suppose to hear.

"What, what did I just walk in on?" I nosed in wondering what it was now that I did that had them whispering behind my back. I was starting to begin to think my house was a magnet for secrets and the world of the fucked up.

"It was nothing, Beth just thinks she knows everything," Tyler growled as he got up from the sofa and looked down on Beth with an evil sneer.

"No, Tyler thinks he know everything and he doesn't know shit!," Beth retorted in aggravation switching her glance from me to Tyler.

"Either someone's going to tell me what's really going on or we can just all shut up and go out to eat." I was in no mood to listen to them bicker, I just wanted dinner over with so I could retreat back to the little bit of peace I maintained when I was left in my solitude.

Beth and Tyler stopped arguing and we all left in Tyler's silver Nissan Xterra. No one spoke another word the entire drive to dinner.

We ended up going to Cassy's Diner fifteen minutes down the street and I ordered a salad with some grilled chicken. I just wanted a plain garden salad but Tyler forced me to add the meat since I had dropped so much weight. Everybody seemed to be more calm now forgetting about the earlier argument that happened before we left out. I was still curious as to what it was about so I figured I'd just ask Beth later when we got some time alone.

I sat there toying with my salad taking minimal bites but Tyler called me out on it, "Do I need to feed da wittle baby," he gibberishly taunted basically warning me I better eat.

"Hey Tyler why don't you move in a little closer to Beth for me," and then I pulled out my phone holding it up like I was ready to take a picture.

"Why?" They both simultaneously asked.

"For your Tinder profile that I'm about to make listing you guys as swingers looking for open relationships," I retorted deadpanned to Tyler's remark trying to keep the mood on a more playful level and to draw away the attention I had garnished for still not eating. Beth and Tyler just ended up chuckling but I could see Tyler had caught on to my diversion shortly after lowering his smile and then gazing onto my plate.

I was too depressed to care about food or anything else. I just wanted to get back into my bed closing my eyes so I could try to forget about Jayce who was always in my thoughts. I think I missed his kisses the most, they were so moist like a ripe strawberry freshly picked and sweet and tender going down making you want to savor the taste for as long as possible.

"Mom eat!" Tyler demanded affirmatively.

I didn't argue or come up with any more witty lines. I figured the longer I bullshitted the longer we would be there keeping me away from my seclusion.

Halfway through my meal I decided it was time for a bathroom break, "I'll be right back, I need to hit the potty."

"Don't take long or Tyler's going to come drag your ass out of the ladies room to make sure you finishing eating," Beth teasingly threatened.

Tyler gave me an imperious look, "She's right you know I will," and then nodded his head downwards dropping his chin to his chest but never unlocked his eyes from mine.

"Yes I do," I said letting out a small laugh. If there was one thing about Tyler it was that he was one brazen son of a bitch not afraid to embarrass me or himself.

I was almost to the bathroom and then I heard the familiar voice that I had been longing to hear once more, "Mia?"

I turned around and there he was with light stubbles of hair partially covering up his devilishly handsome young face and his sparkling crystal blue eyes which locked into me like a heat seeking missile that nothing could break away. His face was hidden under a navy blue baseball cap standing there in short sleeved black polo and blue jeans looking under groomed from his normal appearance but still I couldn't help but find him irresistible.

"Jayce," I uttered his name stupefied frozen in a catatonic state. Of course the one time I finally leave the house I end up going out to eat at the same place Jayce would be.

"Mia, please don't runaway. I love you and I know you love me. Tyler needs to understand that and you need to stop letting him get in the way of us. If I thought you were better off without me I would leave you alone but you're not. Beth's told me how you never eat and hide in your bed all day. You look so unhealthy right now, let me fix you, let me fix us," his words spoken with such gentleness and kindness as he took my hand pulling me in closer. The small tears began to trickle down my cheeks. I was tired of fighting, I was too weak, I wanted to fall into his arms and feel his heat giving me warmth once again and I did. His body emanated onto mine bringing some comfort once more finding myself in his masculine hold.

"I love you too Jayce, I've been such a mess not being able to be with you. I'm just so scared," I looked into his eyes sobbing lost with him, lost without him and then my head started to lower back down in misery.

Jayce took his finger swiping away my tears smoothly making contact with my face as I trembled from his absent touch and then he cupped my chin bringing back up my faltering eyes to meet his gaze.

"I missed my hot Dora," he teased cracking a closed smile and then brought his lips into mine but not before I could let out a small grin. My lips reveled under his remembering that burning passion we once shared slowly bringing me back to life. I couldn't break away as I started running my fingers through his thick dark locks grasping on completely forgetting Tyler was sitting just around the corner.

"Tyler don't!" I heard Beth yell out as I turned to see him pulling away from her while she tried tugging at his arm to keep him from coming towards Jayce and me but she was no match for his strength.

Tyler briskly approached Jayce with a look of vengeance ready to murder anyone who stood in his way.

"Mia let me handle this," Jayce warned while he broke away from our hold pushing me off so I stood behind him.

Fear overtook me leaving me speechless as I could only contemplate how poorly this might end. Jayce was fit and strong but Tyler held some kind of superhuman strength when he was provoked the wrong way turning him into an unstoppable beast. I didn't want either one of them to win or lose beating each other into a pulp, I just wanted all of this fighting to end. Then what happens if they do get out of hand? The police would be called and both of them would end up in jail. Jayce was going off to eventually work with his father so a blemish on his record would do nothing to his career but it could ruin Tyler's entire life.

"What the hell do you think you're doing?' Tyler vented exhaling rapidly with his face just inches away from Jayce's. It was like I was watching a WWE match getting ready to take place but without the bad acting.

"When will you get over yourself? You had nothing to do with us meeting, will you ever get that? I know Mia's tried to tell you and Beth's told me she's even tried to talk to you but your too fucking pigheaded and stubborn. Doe's your mom really look like she's doing okay? You need to open your eyes and see that she loves you so much she'd rather live in her own hell then take the chance of disappointing you over her own happiness. It's killing her literally and your letting her because you're fucking selfish!"

Jayce tried lecturing Tyler with reason while he stood prepared for the unknown.

"Go to hell Jayce! I should kick your ass right here!" I think Tyler finally recognized some truth in Jayce's words only knowing how to reply with his fists as his defense. Tyler moved in ready to pounce and I knew that was my cue to jump in and try to separate them once again.

We now had everyone at the diner just staring at us as I moved in front of Jayce shoving him behind me, "Stop this! Just stop it damn it!" I screamed out but then felt my knees give out from under me. All of I sudden everyone and everything faded to black while I fell weakened to the floor.

"Mia, Mia!" I heard everyone calling out frantically right before there were no sounds at all.

CHAPTER 16

My eyes started to peer slightly open taking in my surroundings. From what it looked like I was at Greater Baltimore Medical Center which I recognized immediately from the window view since that was where I had given birth to Tyler. I could see Charles Street with it's busy daily traffic as I lay in bed with an IV and monitors connected feeling a little woozy. When I looked over in the other direction there besides me was Tyler seated in the hospital chair with his head lying down on crossed arms on the side of my bed resting. His manly snores awaking me as I gazed upon him watching him sleep.

I started leafing my fingers through his thick brown hair with his freckled face lowered trying not to wake him but his head slowly raised up awakened by my touch.

"Mom?" he called to me lifting his head with his eyes swelled and puffy like he had been crying, something he rarely ever did.

"Hey baby," I let out under my breath moving my hand down to his face gently caressing his cheek with my fingers. My beautiful boy looked so sad waking from his sleep. It made me wish I could just cradle him in my arms giving him a kiss to make him feel better like when he was little. I had heard on the radio that a recent pole said mommy kisses actually made things worse but I'll still never believe that.

"I'm sorry for doing this to you letting you get so depressed your fainting because you can't even eat. I just don't know how to accept this. You know, you and Jayce," his voice became sullen as he stared down to the dotted tiled floor.

"Tyler I love him, he makes me happy. I need you to be okay with that," it was time for me to start standing up for myself. I knew now I wasn't going to lose our bond over my relationship with Jayce but a new revolution occurred. Things would never work if Tyler and Jayce couldn't find a common ground and put their differences aside. There couldn't be this constant undying tension between the two of them if Jayce and I were to have a future. I couldn't continually be worried that every time they were together in the same room that one of them would erupt on the other like an exploding volcano ready to scorch everything in it's path.

Before we could further the conversation a knock came at the door with it slowly gaping open as Jayce walked in from behind.

He ignored Tyler's presence looking over to me smiling a delicate grin like I was the only one who could bring such joy to his face. My cheeks grew flushed so enamoured that someone so perfect would gaze upon me with such admiration.

Tyler moved up from his seat with a grunt of dissatisfaction that he made no qualms of concealing and then leaned over my bed giving me a heartfelt hug.

"I'm going to go now. We can talk later, love you," Tyler spoke placing a peck on my forehead before leaving.

"Love you to," and then he pulled back from me striding towards the door giving Jayce a quick look of discontent before he completely made his way out.

"I see he's finally loosening up to you, you're still breathing," I joked with a chuckle.

"Glad to see you still have your sense of humour beautiful," and then Jayce took the empty seat besides me that Tyler had just been in. Without hesitation he took my hand in his leaning over. Before he sat he brushed my hair off to the side with his other coddling my cheek with his firm fingers bringing himself in for a simple kiss. My eyes closed and I took in a deep exhale taking in his touch I had so longingly missed. In an instance those absent butterflies that fluttered inside had been restored.

"I know you know already what brought you here. You were malnutritioned but the doctor said you should be okay to go home in a couple of hours. You just have to be watched over and you have to start eating again. I told the doctor and Tyler you're coming home with me so I can make sure you get better." Jayce said with assertion defiant that I wasn't leaving this hospital with anyone else but him.

"But...." Jayce cut me off not letting me continue even though I really didn't know what I was going to say. I liked the idea of staying with him but I was just surprised Tyler was okay with it.

"Tyler wanted you to stay at the house with him but I told him I'm taking you to my apartment. Beth just left to go back to your house and get some things together for you so you have some clothes to wear. She'll be back in a little bit with your stuff," he spoke sternly like I had no say in the matter. I wasn't going to complain though.

"And Tyler was good with me staying with you?" I gave him the most quizzical baffled look of astonishment.

"Of course not, it's Tyler." Jayce let out a laugh, " We definitely butted heads for a while but Beth helped convince him that it's probably the best thing for you. If it weren't for Beth I think we would have been arguing all night as to who you were going home with. He's not really happy with the idea but he's agreed. "

"I'm glad he's starting to listen to some reason." It was music to my ears knowing I was going to be able to spend time with Jayce once more, even it if was only going to be for a little while. When I got better we were all going to need to sit down and get things settled once and for all. I'd enjoy my time with Jayce and when I got back home I would make my final decision based on how the conversation with the both of them goes and if everyone was still alive.

With everything finally slowly unraveling and becoming less stressful I was starting to feel my appetite come back. "I'm hungry, can you call Beth and try to catch her? I'm in the mood for some Taco Bell. Maybe she can pick some up on the way back."

Jayce reached in his pocket pulling out his phone grinning deviously, "Should I ask her to pick up your backpack and map too since your embracing your Dora side right now?"

"Ouch," Jayce called out as I leaned over in the bed and punched him in his shoulder giving him an evil growl for his smart ass remark.

"You think your so cute don't you?" I grimaced.

"Yup and so do you," he smirked and then he got up from the chair and sat down besides me on the bed. I took my hand to his face and gently caressed the side with my fingers softly rubbing.

"I missed you," he said speaking gingerly and moved in cupping my face in his hands placing the phone down on the medical tray. Taco Bell could wait.

"I missed you," I replied as our lips came in meeting suckling and lapping our tongues to taste one another before letting them entwine.

I ruffled my fingers through his hair which I loved doing and with my other hand I brought it underneath the back of his shirt massaging his backside. His skin felt warm against the flesh of my fingers with those electrical sparks traveling through my insides. I was melting once again practically dissolved underneath his presence as those tiny butterflies fluttered bringing me to some long needed conciliation. I had been so lost without him now starting to find myself again.

I don't know how long our lips stayed locked but I know they didn't seem to want to break away until we were interrupted by the nurse, "Ehem, I need to take a couple more blood samples before we can discharge you," she looked over to us with the glass vials in her hand.

"I'll go out in the hallway and call Beth real quick. What do you want to eat?" Jayce asked pulling away smirking in content like he was feeling the same peace of mind I was.

"Chicken burrito with a Sprite."

Jayce picked his phone back up and exited out into the halls while the nurse came in closer ready to take what she needed.

The nurse took her samples and then Jayce came back in with Beth showing up fifteen minutes later.

"Told you that you needed to eat Sleeping Beauty," it was just like Beth to greet me with a lecture as soon as she arrived.

"Nice to see you too," I rolled my eyes.

Beth stuck around for a little while and left just as I was being discharged. It turns out the conversation I had walked in on earlier between her and Tyler was about Jayce. Apparently she had also been making several efforts to talk some sense into my stubborn child whenever I wasn't around. I just hoped her secret conversations weren't in made in vain and did some good. Tyler was folding but he hadn't been broke.

After the hospital we got to Jayce's apartment and he carried me straight off to the bedroom laying me down as he stood before me.

"Hhhhmmm, does thing mean sex?" I already knew the answer but I figured it was still worth the effort. Of course I missed Jayce because I loved him but I also loved and missed the things he could do to my body.

"You need to get better first. I'd probably break your frail ass you're so thin right now," he said stripping down to his boxers not making things easier for me.

"Fine," I pouted and then undressed myself down to only my panties to get more comfortable tossing my garments to the floor.

"Don't think saying no to you is easy for me. I want to make sure you're healthy before I take advantage of you," he grinned leaning in giving me a kiss on my cheek. "Besides that should give you motivation to get healthier faster."

"Sex is surely a reason to get better," I smiled.

Jayce got into bed lifting the blanket over us and wrapped me in his arms. I let my head fall into his bare chest relishing being in his arms as my body pressed against his heated warmth. I can't believe I gave this up and was considering doing it again but eventually this war between him and Tyler had to come to an end. I just didn't know if I could handle losing Jayce once more. I brushed the negative thoughts aside and let myself enjoy the moment curling myself into him tighter.

"I love you," he uttered kissing the top of my head.

"I love you too," I replied before closing my eyes and going to sleep for the first time in weeks without that emptiness hollowed in my chest.

CHAPTER 17

I was really unhappy with the last chapter I posted. It wasn't where I really wanted to go with the story and I think my hormones and a few beers got the best of me when I wrote it. This is more of what I wanted to do with this chapter and I apologize for the inconvenience as I've removed the other one.

"Wake up gorgeous, time to for breakfast," Jayce came strolling into the bedroom carrying a tray of food dressed only in plaid green boxers with his muscles flexed. Fuck, he was killing me standing practically naked exposing his contoured abs and ripped biceps. I may have been weak but I'm sure I could find some inner strength to ravage him out of those Calvin Klein's my hormones had gone to long without gratification.

"Are you on the menu?" I wickedly asked gawking bringing my eyes down to his boxers as I sat up from bed holding the blanket up with one hand above my breasts with my back pressed up against the pillow. I was so happy to be back with him I had a new found energy and spirit springing out from inside. I also really missed sex.

"Eat, no sex yet until your healthy," he demanded with his eyes seared onto my wilting figure handing me the tray and then took the empty spot next to me on the bed trying to ignore my flirtatious attempt. Couldn't hurt to try right?

"Jayce my love, in all seriousness if you cooked this then I'm not eating it," I tilted my head looking down at the plate with question. It was toast, 2 strips of bacon and scrambled eggs and looked well prepared but if I tasted egg shells I would literally spit it out and lose my entire appetite. From my first and only cooking experience with him I didn't hold much confidence in his talent in the kitchen. This was something I was going to have to teach him how to do right while I was here unlike his sexual skills which he honed in on obviously sometime long before I came along.

"No," he chuckled nudging in closer to me, "there's a place around the corner that opens early and delivers breakfast. I ordered the food while you were still sleeping. I didn't want to wake you it was so early."

"Where's your plate?" I asked admiring his addictive smile that made the corner of my mouth lift up just a little unable to refrain from reciprocating my own small grin.

"I already ate, I got up early this morning and couldn't fall back asleep. I guess I'm still in shock that you're actually here and Tyler's finally starting to come around. It would be nice if we could get back to being friends again even though I know it's not going to happen overnight." His voice lowered sounding a little depressed bringing his head down.

I had just started eating only taking in a few bites and then I placed my fork back down onto the tray. My arms and hands lowered in front of me with my underarms pressed to my sides keeping the blanket still in tact feeling my appetite decreasing. I felt enthralled almost blushing that Jayce couldn't even sleep because I was here but I felt guilt for causing such a riff in between him and Tyler's friendship.

"Hey, this isn't your fault. Don't let this get you down our your never going to get better." He reached under my chin lifting it up so my eyes met his, "Did you hear me, this isn't your fault?" He tried reassuring me as he placed his other hand on top of one mine rubbing soothingly.

"You know if this is going to work between us it's not only Tyler's acceptance that I need? You two have to be able to get along and hopefully mend things back to the way they were." Things were going so well but I couldn't let myself completely forget the open wounds that needed to be healed.

"Snap out of it!" Jayce raised his voice speaking stiffly. "Things are finally falling into place and you're looking to much into it, it's going to get you sick again," he brought his hand down from my face to the tray lifting the fork up with some eggs and brought it to my mouth. "Now eat your breakfast and stop worrying yourself," her persisted with concern.

He was right, I was letting my racing thoughts get the best of me like I so seldom do. I blocked everything out letting myself enjoy being catered to and fed as I opened my mouth in compliance taking in the eggs.

"So what next master?," I teased finishing up my food as Jayce pulled the tray away and sat it off to the side on his dresser before he came back over to the bed.

"We're going out today," he looked over to raising his brows giving me a devilish grin.

I hadn't really thought about it until he just said something but we could actually go out in public for the first time without the fear of being discovered. No more hiding, no more paranoia, I could just go out and appreciate us without having to look over my shoulder.

"Where are we going?," I got excited.

"I had Beth pack your bathing suit, I figured we could go down to Six Flags since it's only forty minutes away. It's about time you got out and had some real fun," he smirked.

I started smiling cheek to cheek at the idea. I loved the thrill you got from roller coasters especially the Superman. I was afraid of heights but yet it was such a rush to drop down from towering heights at fast speeds giving me a natural high and then we could finish up the hot day with a dip in the water.

"I love it," I wrapped my arms around his neck glowing as I gave him a kiss. "When are we leaving?"

"Go get washed up and then we can head out."

I sprung up from bed grabbing my things and went off to the shower with Jayce laughing in the background admiring my innocence. I was like a kid on Christmas waking up to see the bottom of the tree filled with presents.

When we got to the amusement park Jayce took my hand in his entwining our fingers while we walked. There came those butterflies again as I secretly blushed inside things were so surreal and amazing. I was walking in public with the man I loved while he showed his affection without a care in the world.

We spent the day getting on all the rides and he even won me a stuffed Bugs Bunny doll. It was hard to try to contain my flush reddening face I couldn't stop grinning the entire time finding myself in such a peaceful bliss.

We ended the evening in the giant wave pool staying by the shallow end but did minimal swimming. Most of the time I had my legs wrapped around his waist holding onto him while we kissed with my body perched up in his arms. More like the whole time but who needed to swim when I could making out with the man of my dreams?

When we got back to his apartment there was still one thing missing, "Jayce," I called to him as we entered his home standing in the living room.

"What's up Mia?" His glimmering blue eyes beseeching me.

"I know you said you didn't think I was ready but I need you to make love to me," I desperately pleaded longing to truly feel the full extent of his touch once more. I couldn't stand the fact that I was with him but yet I wasn't confined to so many rules like I was a child. I might have not been physically at 100% but I knew my limits and I needed him to see that.

He said nothing, he just brushed a loose strand of my hair behind my ear and started kissing me passionately. I crossed my arms lifting my shirt over my head temporarily separating our lips but only for a brief moment. Thank you, if there was anything besides food that was going to help me get back to myself it was being with him and I mean really being with him.

Jayce swept me up into his arms and carried me off into the bedroom. He placed me down so I stood facing the front of the bed with his face to my back caressing the crook of neck with moist lips."I love you Mia," he whispered.

"Mmmm," I moaned as his tongue slid around with his lips kissing and suckling from behind. His fingers trickled up the sides of my waist moving in towards my breasts sending crashing waves to current through my body.

I moved my hands over top of his massaging my breasts over the cotton of my bra. "God I've missed your touch," I called out with my head tilting back and my eyes rolling back.

"I've missed touching you," he tenderly spoke taking his hands back to undo my bra as his mouth moved down the spine of my back sending earth defying shivers coursing completely through me.

He never stopped kissing and licking down my back while he took one hand to the front of my panties sliding his fingers in the seams until they met my fold rubbing back and forth with slow but steady speed. I grew wetter and wetter under his fingers as he fondled me between my legs causing my breath to hitch hastily.

"Lay down baby," his husky voice lowered as he pressed gently down on the middle of my back guiding me onto the bed with my front side towards the sheets.

I lay there patiently waiting as I listened to him remove his clothing until I felt him hover down above me removing my panties.

He position his body straddled over top of mine with his knees pressed against the mattress sitting down below the outsides of my hips.

Once more his fingers fell down to my fold rubbing while he slipped a finger into my depths. I tingled all over as he pumped his finger into me adding another gliding in and out preparing me for what I had been craving.

"Are you ready?" He asked as I shook beneath him fervently yearning for sacrilege.

"Yes Jayce, I'm ready," I replied laying there with my eyes closed and my hands above the bed with my fingers clinging to the sheets.

I felt himself lead his manhood into me as he leaned down kissing onto my shoulder. Gracefully he entered thrusting while he placed his hands over top of mine still caressing my backside licking and making small bites. I relished the feel of him laying above as he continually thrusted back and forth with increasing force.

My skin felt like it was on fire burning with lust as he moved in and out bringing his face over to meet my lips. He kissed me roughly taking my face in his hand as the hammering became more harsh but not without merit giving me intense pleasures that were making my toes about the curl.

We panted and moaned gasping for breath locked into one another until that one hard thrust hit igniting off fireworks.

"Mia, I don't want to pull out, I want to keep going," he struggled to speak.

"It's okay, I'm on the pill now. You don't have to stop," I offered enjoying him inside of me even if I had already met my peak.

His body gyrated and thrusted several more times until he moaned out in contentment then dropped down lifelessly on top of me.

"I've really missed that," his words spoken right below my ear while I felt his heated breath emanate against my skin still having the power to cause me to shudder.

"So have I," I replied.

CHAPTER 18

We were sprawled out on the his white leather couch with me nestled above him relaxing in the mid afternoon watching a movie when Jayce decided to sneak in the compromising situation into a conversation, "My sister Andrea is home for a couple of days and she's staying with my dad right now. They're having dinner tonight and I want you to come with me and meet them." He mentioned nonchalantly not looking away from the tv screen to put on the facade that this wasn't an uncomfortable position he was putting me in .

My body tensed up in his hold as I turned my head to meet his ocean eyes, "I don't know if I'm ready for all that. What if they don't like me or think I'm just some skanky cougar who likes to molest young handsome men?" I felt so uneased by the idea of meeting his family. What if they disapproved of the two of us? It would just totally make me feel like shit.

"Mia," Jayce chuckled staring at me with extreme sincerity stroking my arm with his hand, "They'll love you just like I do and we're both of legal age."

"How bout next time Andrea comes home I meet them?" I put on a cheesy smile knowing damn well I was going to lose this battle.

"How bout you meet them tonight," he said giving me a stern glance and then placed a gently kiss on my lips.

"Oh that's right I forgot, I'm have to go into the office tonight. One of the servers are down and they need me to take care of it," the cheesy smiled glimmered again across my face.

"You can bullshit all you want but your coming," Jayce assured me knowing that he was going to come out victorious the smug bastard but so adorable and sexy.

"Fine. What time are we leaving?" I questioned rolling my eyes bringing my chin down to my chest with a deep sigh wanting to have time to prepare and look my most presentable since first impressions were the most lasting.

"We'v e got 2 hours."

"Shit! I need to start getting ready now," I exclaimed jumping up to my feet startling him from my abrupt actions.

"Mia calm down, you have time to get ready," Jayce ignorantly replied not knowing how much time it took a woman to prepare for such an event.

"No, you don't understand! I need to start getting ready now," I hastily insinuated standing in front of him shaking and frantic.

Jayce reached out taking my hand in his and kissed my palm putting me in a weakened state, "Everything is going to be fine," His head nodded down in assurance. "Go get ready and do all that girly stuff you do and stop freaking out."

Easy for him to say, he wasn't the milf that bedded her prey but I complied without argument and headed to the bedroom.

I first went to the closet where some of my dresses were hanging and stood there for at least 10 minutes trying to figure out which one was the most presentable and at the same time made me look good and feel good about myself. I decided on my pink satin dress with string straps that had red floral prints. (Yes I know. I liked string strapped and floral print but they seemed to suit me well.)

I pulled my dress out and hung it up on the closet knob as I made my way to the bathroom to shower. A fresh yellow towel sat hanging on the wall on the rod ready for me as I set the wetness to the right degree. I then entered the basking waters letting the pellets calm my nerves after I quickly undressed.

As soon as my body stood underneath the steamy waterfall I became unraveled and lost under the downpour. The shower was my escape from reality giving me calmness and comfort caressing my naked body letting me forget about the world outside of the soothing waters.

"Mia!" Jayce stormed into the bathroom. "You've been in there for an hour! You need to get ready." He stood behind the clear doors ready to pull me out and dress me himself I had let my body and mind drift away. I had become too relaxed forgetting the disturbing issues that had been running through my head causing me to lose track of time.

"Fine, fine. I got cha," I stepped out removing the cotton towel off the hanging rack. I dried my body off placing it around me and grabbed another off the wall wrapping it firmly around my soaking wet hair making my way out to the bedroom.

I reached into Jayce's top dresser where I had been keeping my undergarments and pulled out some panties and a bra slipping them on as I undid the towels letting them falter to the carpeted floor. Then I made my way over to my hanging dress taking it off the knob slipping my body underneath once it was removed from the hanger. The worry of disapproval began to flood through me once again as I stared into the mirror looking down on myself.

"Jayce, I can't do this. Maybe I can meet your family during Christmas break instead?" I asked still looking at my reflection now shivering nervously terrified of rejection from the most important people in Jayce's life.

Jayce came up from behind me placing his rigid oversized hands on my shoulders and gingerly began to rub up and down my arms from behind. I closed my eyes rejoicing under his touch slowly beginning to calm down as his fingers massaged my flesh. His wet lips gently met with the arch of my neck with a soft succulent kiss distracting me from racing thoughts.

Briefly I opened my eyes admiring his strong build and thick biceps through the mirror. Mine, he was all mine, I exhaled a deep breath of content.

"Stop freaking out beautiful. You have nothing to worry about," he whispered as I felt his hot breath hit onto the skin below my ear helping to ease my unsettled nerves.

"Damn it! You make it so impossible to say no to you. You know that right?" I replied dissolving under his caresses.

"Yea, I know," he lifted his head so our eyes would meet in the mirror with a devious smirk planted across his face. "Now finish getting ready," and then he dropped his hands from my arms smacking my ass before he walked away to get prepared himself.

While Jayce washed up and dressed I dried off my hair brushing it out straight so that my long black locks ran smoothly down my back and lightly applied some make-up. I didn't want to overdo myself and come off looking like some painted hooker.

When we were both ready we got into Jayce's SUV taking the 20 minute drive that felt more like seconds I felt so unprepared as to what was to come.

His father's house was magnificent and quite large painted all white with green shutters. Not as big as a mansion but not much smaller as it stood with a striking landscaped lawn filled with sculpted bushes and blooming flowers leading up the centered driveway.

We parked directly out front making our way in through the double doors with my body nervously trembling once again as Jayce help my hand tightly for comfort.

"Hello Mia. Nice to finally meet you," a handsome older man met us at the door extending a formal hand out to me as the front doors shut behind us. I immediately knew he was Jayce's father by the similar striking features his son obviously inherited. He was tall and thick like his son with dark satin hair that was slightly graying but it didn't take away from his wickedly good looks one bit. At least now I knew what Jayce would look like with age if we lasted and it was far from disappointing.

"Nice to meet you too Mr. Montgomery," I complied reaching out to shake his hand.

"Please, call me Neal," What was I thinking? He was probably closer in age to me then his son and I was calling him Mister. I could have seriously bitch slapped my dumb ass for that one. Way to go Mia, your molesting his son and making him feel like the old one. He so probably hates me already.

"Yes of course," I forced a smile from my embarrassment as our hands pulled away.

"Hey dad," Jayce stepped in greeting his father with a hug. "Where's Andrea?"

"She's waiting for you both in the living room." Neal replied turning around and walking as we followed behind.

We entered the exquisite room that was furnished with a large red sectional sofa and recliner with a fireplace sitting at the end and glass tables surrounding them. On the couch sat a gorgeous platinum blonde young woman with a curvy figure and blue glassy eyes that seared right through me. She looked nothing like Jayce but she was attractive in her own right probably getting her good looks from mother who I'm sure had to beautiful producing such attractive children.

"Hi. You must be Andrea," I greeted walking in with a smile but she turned to me with no words sneering and then looking back away. I knew this wasn't going to be easy.

"Andrea!" Jayce's deep voice raised in anger,"Be nice," he looked upon her demandingly tightening his grip on my hand as our fingers still lay entwined with one anothers.

"It's okay Jayce," I stepped in turning my head to meet his eyes knowing that I wasn't going to be easily accepted considering our age difference.

"No it's not. She has no right to be so rude to you,"Jayce defiantly persisted as Andrea still sat there quiet with her head veered away from our direction bearing a disgruntled look.

"Jayce why don't you go out and grab some wine for dinner and I'll go help the cook prepare dinner while these two get acquainted," Neal cut in relieving some of the tension.

"Okay," Jayce replied still bitter but walked away towards the door with keys in hand right after giving me a small peck on my lips. "I'll be back soon Mia, don't let her scare you," he told me glancing at his sister with an evil dissatisfied look as he opened up the door to walk out.

I just nodded a look of I'll be okay not wanting to say something that would stir up more trouble. Jayce accepted my response and left without more argument.

Neal left Andrea and me along in the living room as I took a seat adjacent to her on the recliner as soon as Jayce exited the house.

Before my butt had a chance to get warm on the cushion underneath me Andrea spurted out her objections to my relationship with her brother, " I don't like you. You know that right? I know you're just using my brother because he's good looking and our father has money. You're just an older desperate woman looking for her prize," Her mesmerizing eyes now turning grey with coldness as she stared at me with hatred.

"I'm truly sorry you think that because you honestly have the wrong idea. I do well enough on my own and I don't really care much for materialistic things. I love Jayce. He's never bought me anything expensive and I don't want him too. He knows I prefer the simpler things in life and would be offended if I felt he was trying to buy me. Yes I am older but somehow we just click. I hope you'll be able to see that," I tried being assuring but I could see no matter what I said would help my case when it came to her. I couldn't blame her though. If I was in her shoes I would probably think the same question an older woman with such a younger man.

"Jayce will come to his senses," she replied snickering as she turned her attention to the wall with a blank stare.

I didn't bother trying to defend myself again as we sat there in silence awaiting either Neal to come back in or Jayce to return home to break us out of the uncomfortable situation.

10 minutes went by with no one to come in and save me as we sat distanced with no words spoken until the home phone went off ringing.

Andrea got up from her seated position and picked up the cordless phone from the table behind the couch, "Hello?" She curiously answered apparently not recognizing the number on the caller id.

I watched as her faced turned a pale white with someone on the other end obviously saying something horrific from the expressions on her face.

"Where is he at?" She screamed violently apparently shaken up from what she was hearing.

That emptiness that burrowed in your stomach when you could sense something was extremely wrong pitted inside of me desperate for answers.

"What's going on?" I yelled out in concern jumping up from my seat.

"We have to go. Jayce has been in an accident," she replied frantically and then screamed out, "Dad! Come on, Jayce was in a car accident!" She swiped her car keys off of the corner table as Neal came running into the room.

"Andrea what happened?" he worriedly asked clasping onto her shoulders with fear and concern burning in his eyes looking deep into her for answers.

"I don't know dad but we need to leave," I could see the tears starting to stream down her cheeks as mine did the same.

We got into Andrea's Toyota Prius as my body quaked in the back seat only fearing the worst.

CHAPTER 19

Andrea raced to the scene of the accident like she was driving in a Nascar sprint cup which I couldn't be more thankful for. If I had been driving I would have drove just as fast needing to know if Jayce was okay.

My body shook profusely in fear that I could lose him if I already hadn't but somehow those undeniable senses that peaked in inconspicuously convinced me that he was alright but the tears still flowed down my cheeks.

Andrea pulled up to the accident with ambulances and fire trucks surrounding. I immediately saw Jayce seated on a stretcher in the back of an emergency vehicle on the stretcher.

Before the car was completely stopped I unbuckled myself and flung the door open jumping out of the passenger side without haste. I ran to the red and white lighted vehicle ignoring the paramedic besides Jayce checking his vitals. My arms swung around his neck as my lips kissed all over his face frantically relieved that he was alive.

"Jayce! I was so worried you weren't going to be okay. I don't think I could handle losing you again, at least not like this. I love you so much." My lips kept pressing against his face with the realization that he might have never been in my arms again.

"Mia I'll never leave you I swear. I love you too and could never leave you alone," His fingers leafed through my hair as his eyes locked into mine with nothing but true love intensely scouring into me.

"Are you okay? What happened?" I asked in concern placing another peck on his forehead as my hands ruffled and pulled through his short dark locks sitting besides him on the stretcher.

"It was just a fender bender, I'm fine baby," He complied taking my cheek into his hand as he brought his lips onto mine licking across my bottom one as his teeth took it in with a gentle nibble. I felt his tongue swipe above demanding entrance into my mouth as his overpowering dominance took way taking over my lips and tongue.

"Don't ever scare me like this again," I asserted pulling away from his lips pressing my wet face into his shoulder hugging him dearly and then Andrea and Neal's voices made way.

"Jayce oh my god! You had me so scared!" Andrea called out pushing me aside and wrapping her arms around Jayce's neck taking my place.

"Son, you had us all worried," Neal's eyes teared like a true loving father as he stood there in relief but still shaken by the whole ordeal.

"Everything's fine, you don't have anything to worry about you guys. I'm okay and I'm not dying."

"Well I'm not letting you out of my sight for the rest of the night!" I commanded.

I looked over to Andrea expecting her to intervene but she didn't. She just sat there quietly with no issues.

"Okay Mia, I've got it. We can go back to my dad's and you can watch over me and see that I'm perfectly fine and stop worrying," Andrea had already released her hold on him standing off to the side of the stretcher while Jayce pulled me back in close.

"I'll go wherever you want me to as long as you're there," I was ready to say yes to anything he asked as long as I was with him to know he was safe after such a scare.

"Give me a second Mia to talk to my sister and dad," Jayce spoke taking my hand gently into his.

"Alright," I agreed pulling away and exiting the ambulance taking a nervous stance along the sides.

"I love you Mia," Jayce called before letting go of my hand not caring what Neal and Andrea thought.

"I love you too," I responded forgetting about all the people around us.

Impatiently I awaited until Andrea walked up to me on the side of the emergency vehicle. "I don't apologize often but when I'm wrong I'm wrong. The way you acted when you heard Jayce got into an accident wasn't fake. You do really care for my brother and I can see that now. I'm sorry for misjudging you," Andrea sincerely apologized.

"It's okay, I can see where you were coming from. I'm just glad you can see that I really do love him and I'm not trying to take advantage. Jayce is amazing and he makes me happy in a way I thought was never possible," I knew from the expression on her face not much more needed to be said.

Andrea walked away with a small smile from my response as I made way back to the inside of the truck where Jayce sat. Neal had apparently left also leaving me alone with Jayce still seated on the bed.

I patiently waited as the paramedics finished checking Jayce out and cleared him to leave. We all had to take Andrea's car back as Jayce's truck was left undrivable having to be towed.

The entire way back I sat silently in the back Jayce by my side with my head rested on his shoulder and my arm wrapped tightly around his waist.

When we got back to the house we got resettled and had a nice peaceful dinner without the unwanted tension that had occurred earlier between me and Andrea when we first arrived. After dinner Jayce went off with his father and I sat in the living room with his sister.

Andrea and I spoke getting to know each other until Jayce and his father returned and we all chatted for another hour or so until the sun started to go down.

"It's starting to get late. I think Mia and I should start to head out now," Jayce said as me, him, and Andrea sat on the couch while his father sat across from us on the recliner.

"Glad you were able to stop by and it was nice to finally meet you Mia," Neal spoke while we all stood.

"Yea it was nice meeting you Mia," Andrea added in before turning to Jayce giving him a hug.

"Thank you for a lovely dinner and I'm happy I got the opportunity to meet you both," I politely said reaching out shaking Neal's hand in gratitude.

"You're very welcome," Neal complied nodding his head with a smile.

"So little sis, going to give your big brother a ride home?" Jayce asked still in his sister's embrace.

"Of course," and then we all went out to the car after finishing our good-byes with his father heading back to the apartment.

To my surprise when we arrived Andrea got out of the car and gave me a hug assuring me of her approval .Then she moved over to her brother and said her farewells hugging him too before she got back in her vehicle and drove away.

Jayce and I entered his complex making our way up the elevator to his third floor apartment. When we got inside we went straight to the sofa and put on a movie (our daily boring routine when we weren't out and about or having a good time in the bedroom.)

"See that wasn't so bad was it?" Jayce smiled at me as we leaned back on the couch in the living room sitting side by side.

"Oh no, you getting into a car accident was nothing. Being scared out of my witts is always a good day in my books," I replied sarcastically with one eyebrow raised.

"Come here," he chuckled grabbing me by my hips pulling me down onto his chest. With my back pressed against his front side he took one hand to my cheek so I faced him placing a hard rough kiss against my lips. I know I've mentioned it before but God I loved his kisses. They were either soft and gently or harsh and demanding but always executed with preciseness and skill never coming off sloppy and desperate.

With the scare I had today it was another reality check. Losing Jayce wasn't in the cards for me, emotionally the idea tore me to pieces but we still had one more barrier to overcome when it came to him and Tyler. His family was now accepting to me but my family needed to be welcoming also with no conflicts. I knew my parents and sister wouldn't need much winning over but as always Tyler needed to cool off and for good this time. I wasn't looking forward to coming home but the day was nearing.

Jayce's kisses were some what settling shutting me up blocking my fears as we continued locking lips in the living room until the exhaustion kicked in minutes after from all the commotion the day had brought. I fell asleep in his solid arms as we both spent the night sleeping on the sofa never making it to the bedroom.

CHAPTER 20

"**I**f you don't give me back that tv control I'm going to tickle you," Jayce threatened hovering above me on the couch as I lie underneath with the remote under my back.

"I don't want to watch the baseball game right now, I was watching that movie and if you tickle me you will die," I warned deepening my voice and bulging my eyes. He knew I couldn't handle being tickled, it made me go insane to the point I would play dirty just make it stop.

"Please no, stop," I begged giggling while he started in torturing my sensitive sides leaving me squirming underneath his wrath. My body twisted and turned trying to break free but I was no match for strength so I resorted to biting. I sunk my teeth deep into his shoulder no longer able to endure the involuntary twitching that was driving me to go mad.

"Ouch! Okay, okay, you win, I'll stop," Jayce smiled now letting his wild fingers calm bringing one hand up to my face and the other under the seams of my shirt tenderly running his fingers up and down my skin.

"Good," I smirked letting out a giggle and then I bobbed my head up lightly tugging his bottom lip with my teeth and then started suckling until our mouths met and we were kissing.

"Oh, I meant to ask you, when did you go on the pill?" He asked breaking away nudging himself besides me in the cracks of the sofa. He began stroking back my hair with one hand and resting his other on the side of my waist as his arm extended across my stomach.

"I was always on birth control. Some certain someone who unexpectedly showed up at my door with my son and moved himself in immediately had me stressing so bad I kept forgetting to take them. I didn't really have as many distractions around once you left to keep me from remembering to take the pills." I furrowed my brows giving him an evil eye.

"Are you insinuating that I distracted you from your daily routines?" He devilishly smirked.

"Never," I taunted with sarcasm and then I started lifting myself up to a seated position pulling him up with me.

"We have to leave soon," I added in. I was finally going back home after staying with Jayce for almost two weeks. I had started eating again regularly and was beginning to look like my old self once more. I didn't let myself dwell on Tyler and just relaxed and appreciated what me and Jayce had but now it was time to find out if this really could work. Was Tyler going to be willing to move on and stop hating or was he going to inadvertently destroy my happiness?

"You know if Tyler still wants to act like a dick to me I'm not letting you leave me again right? You were miserable when we weren't together and so was I. I'm not going to lose you." He defiantly asserted clasping my cheek in his hand looking into my eyes sternly.

"I love you but I don't think I could deal with worrying every second that something bad might happen. You guys are getting ready to go back to school in a few days and have some of the same courses so you're going to have to be in the same room as each other when I'm not around to watch over you both." That gaping hole that use to sit inside my chest slowly started creeping back in as the realization that things could go so wrong filtered in my head.

"Do you remember what I told you back when this first all started? Tyler loves you and when you truly love someone you want them to be happy. We'll work things out, you'll see." I needed his positive words because my paranoia was starting to strike back in and I was only imaging the worst.

"Okay, I'll text Tyler and let him know we'll be there in about an hour. I want to get washed up real quick first."

"Then I'm getting in the shower with you," his eyes bulged and one side of his lips cringed to the side as his chin met his chest with a look that said it was taking no arguments.

"Whatever," I twisted my head letting my hair wisp back and forth batting my lashes like I didn't want him to join me and then I texted my son real quickly so I could continue with my fun.

With that we speedily made our way to the bathroom halting that emptiness from filling my chest from his distractions.

We bathed and for once I avoided the sex more focused on what was going to come of the day but the shower was still utterly pleasurable. Jayce had lathered up my head running his fingers through my hair gently massaging my scalp sending rhythmic pulsations down to my core. His hands covered every inch of my body soaped up thoroughly cleansing my exterior while my body dissolved under his caress. Never had anyone made my heart beat so rapidly and make my pulse race the way he did but in a good way. We hadn't been together real long but he had my heart in a way no other man ever had. It was going to kill me if I had to give this up.

After we got done cleansing our bodies we got dressed and went to our cars driving separately. I had my car with me while I stayed with Jayce but now playing house was over. It was time to return to the real world and face reality.

The drive was only 10 minutes long but I felt like my entire life was flashing before me like I was ready to die within those brief moments. From the minute Tyler was born to where Jayce came into my life turning my world upside down. Oh God if you're out there I'm going to swear this is the last time I ask you for anything, but hey we know that's not really true. Just work with me though. Please let me have some real happiness in my life and don't take away either of the men I love so dearly in my life. If there really was a heaven above I was making sure they heard my calls because I was scared shitless of my world falling apart once again.

We got to my house and Tyler's Nissan wasn't there. I didn't know if I should take it as a bad thing or a good thing. I had more time to avoid him but was he avoiding me instead? I decided to text him to make sure everything was okay.

Me: I'm home now. Where you at?

Tyler: Was over Ashley's. There was an accident on 695. Be home in 20

Me: Okay be safe love you

Tyler: Will do love you

Me and Jayce had made ourselves comfortable on the couch coddled in each others arm watching tv awaiting Tyler to arrive but the nervousness was sinking in hard.

"I'll be right back," I got up springing from the sofa.

"Where are you going?" Jayce peculiarly asked.

"I just have to go to the bathroom. I'll be back in a minute," I lied. I had a few cigarettes left hidden in my dresser that I was fiending for at the moment needing a smoke to calm my nerves. Jayce totally objected to my smoking which wasn't a regular thing but the stress I was under was craving for a couple of puffs to relieve some tension.

I made my way back downstairs with my pack in hand trying to bullshit a good reason for going outside. I knew if I smoked in the house he would catch me right away even though he would smell the tobacco on me afterwards but if I got outside I would at least be able to get in a couple good of drags in. "I think I need some air right now, I'll be right back." I told Jayce still seated on the sofa as I stood at the bottom of the stairway.

"Mia?" His brows raised looking over to my hand. "What's that you're holding?"

"I don't know what you're talking about," I nonchalantly tried to play off shrugging my shoulders.

"Oh I think you know exactly what I'm talking about," he lifted himself up coming towards me snatching the pack out of my hands.

"Come on Jayce please? Just one." I begged with saddened desperate eyes.

"Only if you can get them from me," he taunted lifting the pack up in the air with his arm held high knowing my 5'4 height could never reach so high.

"Damn it Jayce, give them to me," I pleaded bouncing up and down like a rabbit trying to snatch it out of his hands as he laughed in amusement while I struggled.

Come on Mia can't you reach?" He smirked antagonizing me.

I decided this was like the tickle war, no holds barred as I attempted to cheat my way to victory. I moved my hand down the seams of his jeans and let my fingers glide up and down to only as far as they could reach not being able to pass below an inch or two because his pants were securely buttoned.

"You're never playing fair are you?" His eyes focused into mine dropping the pack and lifting me up so my thighs wrapped around his waist and my arms tightly fit around his neck. He threw me down on the sofa pinning my arms above me. "So what should I do with you?" He asked moving in closer like he was ready to take advantage of my vulnerable state.

At that the we heard the door fling open with Tyler making his way in causing us to jump to a seated position with distance.

Immediately Jayce looked over to Tyler standing up, "Can I talk to you privately in the kitchen?" his voice dropped deep with a serious tone.

"Yea sure," Tyler responded gritting his teeth like he was trying to hold back his disliking of the whole situation but complied.

I wanted to say something but no words could escape me as I was clueless to how I should respond. I just sat back silently while they made their way to the kitchen. It seemed like an eternity waiting in the living room trying to preoccupy myself with games on my phone or tv but nothing could hold my attention while I impatiently awaited their return.

Finally after what was about 20 minutes they both came out. I watched from a far as they both shook hands unable to hear the words they spoke.

Tyler walked over to me after their hands met and leaned in for a loose hug and a kiss on the cheek. "Love you mom, I want you to be happy," and then a small grin cornered on his face.

"Love you too," I smiled hugging him back and placing a small peck on his own cheek.

Tyler went upstairs and I was now left alone with Jayce who moved in taking a seat next to me and wrapping his arm around my shoulder pulling me into his lips. "What did you say to him?" I asked shocked that things went so well.

"We just had a serious discussion on how we both love you and want what's best for you. Let's just leave it t that." Discussion was over as he moved in taking his mouth into mine with a kiss so passionate the world could end and I wouldn't have even noticed.

After that night It took several months and a lot of bickering but after time Tyler and Jayce warmed back up to each other. Little by little Tyler got use to seeing me and Jayce showing intimacy even though he growled and cringed a lot at first. I had the two most amazing men in my life with no more secrets and lies. With Tyler's true acceptance I was finally with the one man I was meant to be with and this time for good. Before Jayce had come along there was always a piece of me missing, an empty void that needed to be filled. Jayce gave me compassion, romance, laughter, love, he gave me life filling that emptiness that every woman needs filled.

I just sat back on the recliner with a glowing sparkle illumi-nating around me as I watched my two favorite men play video games together sat on the sofa. My world was perfect, it was finally complete.

Epilogue

One year later

I woke up this morning worn out from another uninhibited passionate evening with Jayce. Now that he was living at the house with me there was never a dull night in the bedroom. With his youth and my insatiable desires we always found a way to keep ourselves entertained and I loved it, I loved him.

Tyler was now living a few blocks down the street in his own apartment with roommates. He had finally got to the point in his life where he felt it was time to stop living with mommy and daddy. That and he was in the partying stages of his life which thankfully Jayce had never really grown accustomed to. Jayce and I would go out from time to time to get drinks or go dancing and sometimes he would just go out with the guys while I stayed home if they weren't hanging out here. I trusted him and Tyler was always with him ready to kick his ass if he did get out of line, not that there was really a need.

Where the hell was Jayce anyways? I rolled over with my hair all disheveled rubbing my sleepy eyes ready to throw my arm around his stiff solid waist and the space besides me lie empty. Well almost empty. In his spot there was a rolled up piece of paper fastened with a knotted string.

I let out a small giggle curious what he was up to now. I sat up unraveling the sheet and inside was a poorly drawn map done with crayons leading to Jayce's restaurant. His father had given him Harbor Lights, the restaurant we had our first official date that night now long ago. I guess I was going out to find out what he was up to. He was always doing the unpredictable keeping things fun and interesting putting a smile on my face.

I got out of bed and went into the bathroom to wash up and the first thing I noticed was a post-it on the mirror. I leaned over pulling it off as I read what it had to say: Go to the closet

I walked over to find my next surprise unfolding the closet doors and there hung a book bag with another note fastened on the outside causing me to grimace but laugh at the same time. I could see where this was going, the map, the backpack, he never did let up on the Dora jokes ever since I placed that band-aid below his scraped up leg. This note read: Wear me

Inside the bag was a red neatly folded lace embroidered summer dress I had never seen. Now I was getting really excited and more curious to what he was up too with such an elaborate set up put into place.

Hastily I took down the bag removing the dress and laying it out on my bed then hopped in the shower and washed up. When I got out drying off and dressing I made sure I did my hair and makeup to perfection wanting to look my best for him since he had gone to such extremes.

I strided out of the house grabbing my keys off the rack with my purse in hand and got into my little black Corolla heading off towards downtown. It was a wonder I didn't get pulled over by the police I drove like I was trying to make pole position dying to know what Jayce had in store for me.

I drove up stopping right in front being greeted by Samuel, the valet, "Hello Mia, Jayce is inside waiting for you," he said holding the door open for me bowing down and extending his hand out to escort me out of my car like a gentleman.

"Thank you Samuel," I stepped out making my way to the entrance while he took my car away.

When I got inside the place was completely empty except for Michelle the hostess who handed me a menu, "Jayce said to open this," her face garnished a large bright grin.

"Okay," I peculiarly replied taking hold of the menu. I opened it up and of course another note (I should have known better):

Meet me at the balcony

I got to the patio pulling open the white hinged french doors and there was Jayce sharply dressed in a white tuxedo jacket, black bow tie, and finished off with jeans and a pair of Adidas (elegant but simple, that was my Jayce) on one bended knee opening up a petite box with a sparkling princess cut diamond inside.

"Marry me," his radiant blue eyes implored looking up at me, small tears of joy began to falter down my cheeks.

"Yes," I whimpered shaken but thrilled barely getting the words out I was in such shock and admiration.

Jayce stood up placing the the precious gem on my finger bringing his soft pink lips into mine to seal things with an intense kiss that brought me melting like ice in the hot summers heat.

The only thing now missing from our lives was a child of our own.